A Very Civilized Man

A novel by
MARGARET THOMSON DAVIS

Allison & Busby
London

First published in Great Britain 1982 by
Allison and Busby Limited
6a Noel Street, London W1V 3RB

Copyright © 1982 by Margaret Thomson Davis

British Library Cataloguing in Publication Data

Davis, Margaret Thomson
    A very civilized man.
    I. Title
    823'.914 [F]   PR6054.A8926

    ISBN 0-85031-449-6

Set in 10/11pt Imprint by Alan Sutton Publishing Ltd, Gloucester.
Printed in Great Britain by Biddles Ltd, Guildford and King's Lynn.

"What wings are these beating around
my bed in the long silence of the night."

Kahlil Gibran
Prose Poems

Chapter One

ANN TRACED the growth of the confusing maze inside herself to the night before her daughter Helen's marriage. Everything had been perfectly all right until then. She'd known where she was. Admittedly there had been times when she had been accused of being absentminded, a bit of a dreamer and a bookworm.

"You're away in another world half the time," Charlie often told her when she hadn't heard what he'd said in the first place. But there was never any anger in his voice and nothing that she was, or said, or did, affected the solid, familiar path of their marriage. Charlie knew her and she knew Charlie. She'd thought she knew herself. Then the night before Helen's wedding to Dave, while Helen was out for a "hens' party", she had set about cleaning the house and getting everything organized for the big day. She was giving Helen's room a thorough doing out when she came across a pile of letters and cards and two coloured photographs hidden under the mattress of the divan. On top was a scrap of paper with words penned in Helen's neat hand:

> Photographs and memories
> Christmas cards you sent to me
> All that I have, are these
> To remember you. . . .
>
> Photographs and memories
> All the love you gave me
> Somehow it just can't be true
> That's all I've left of you.

A picture of Eric, Helen's last boyfriend, grinned out at her, as startling as ever with his brassy blond hair that stuck up in spikes, and his long gold earring dangling. Another photograph showed Eric and Helen with arms locked around each other. Helen with hair warmly glowing like polished mahogany and large brown eyes, a young replica of her mother. Ann glanced inside one of the envelopes, and although she guessed they were love letters from Eric, she was unprepared for the terms in which that first letter was written. She read it awkwardly without taking it out of the envelope as if not doing so would make it seem less like prying. The shock and distress the letter caused her Ann accepted as a punishment. The tender and loving words in it revealed such a different Eric from the person she'd thought he was, it brought her whole judgement into question and jerked her into having not only a different viewpoint of Eric but of herself.

1

Never for one moment had she taken Eric seriously, regarding him as a "phase" that Helen was going through. She and Charlie used to groan together and roll their eyes and talk about Helen's "punk phase".

Admittedly Helen had seemed terribly upset after her last quarrel with Eric. She'd tried to comfort the girl by saying the usual things: "Don't worry, you'll get over it, dear. . . . You'll meet someone else, you'll see. . . ."

She hadn't reckoned on Helen meeting someone else quite so soon afterwards. Of course, Helen had actually known Dave for some time at work. He was in charge of the "Do-it-yourself Department" at Foyer's and Helen worked in cosmetics.

At first worry had flitted across her mind like a shadow when it occurred to her that Helen might be turning to Dave on the rebound, but the shadow disappeared as quickly as it had come. Dave was such a nice, steady man. The fact that he was a few years older than Helen was all to the good. He drank very little and was all for saving money. Practically everything in his council flat in East Dolton had been made by himself. There would never be any danger of his ill-treating her daughter or keeping her short of money. (Eric had never seemed to have a penny to his name and any money he did make he seemed to lavish on his motor-bike rather than on Helen.) She would be all right with Dave.

In a way, Dave reminded her of Charlie. They didn't look alike. Charlie was massive in comparison with Dave. They were both sturdily built men but Charlie, despite his cropped grey hair, could pass as an all-in wrestler at his peak, while Dave was more wiry like a sandy-haired boxer.

Charlie, like Dave though, was a steady man. Steady as a rock. You could always depend on Charlie. Twenty-five years they'd been married and hardly ever a cross word. As long as Charlie was supplied with the kind of meals he enjoyed and as long as he was allowed to relax in front of the television when he came home from work he was perfectly content and happy. She had no complaints either. She had been kept happily busy with cooking meals for Helen and Charlie, keeping the house nice for them and doing the shopping, and in between times she had her books. She had practically worked her way through the local library. Often she and the librarian had a good laugh about it. "Our best customer" they called her and said: "It's taking us all our time to keep up with you, Mrs Sommerville."

There was nothing she liked better than to curl up, shoeless, on the chair by the fire in a nest of cushions, with a box of chocolates and a packet of cigarettes at her elbow, and lose herself in a book. The afternoon was usually her reading time. It was sheer luxury.

The best time of the day, the time when she felt life was good and she was lucky.

Now, even with her chocolates and her cigarettes and curled deep into her favourite chair, she couldn't completely relax into the imaginary world of her book. A thread of unease held her back and the story only succeeded in skimming over the surface of her attention. It was *Lolita* and she had to hide it from Charlie. Charlie didn't like what he called "dirty books". He was a regular Mary Whitehouse.

But it wasn't thoughts of Charlie that were making her feel too abstracted to read.

The letters and cards and photographs had gone from under the divan. She wondered if Helen had destroyed them. Probably not. Eric, she now realized, had been Helen's first love, and first love affairs were always precious. It was then that, surprisingly, Ann remembered her own. What a man he had been and how she had loved him. Man, did she say? It seemed incredible now to realize that Joel had been only nineteen. Strange how she should find herself, a middle-aged woman, feeling such a pang for a lad of nineteen.

Embarrassed by her own foolishness she tossed the book aside and went to clear out the dirty washing basket and take the clothes through to the washing machine. It was an automatic and a few clicks of a switch soon set it going. As if a switch had clicked on inside herself, she felt compelled to keep on the move. She decided to do her shopping list and then go out to the shops. With a pad and pencil in hand she inspected the spotlessly clean and neatly kept food cupboards, fridge and freezer. She didn't really need anything except perhaps milk and eggs. Although Charlie didn't like cereal and he preferred to put dried milk in his tea. He liked a steaming hot cup and complained that ordinary milk from the fridge cooled it down. She used dried milk because it was skimmed and therefore good for slimming. Helen had always kept an eagle eye on her for that.

"Mum," she'd warn, "don't eat that cake. You'll get all fat and horrible and old-looking. It's only because you keep so slim that you look at least ten years younger than your age."

Not much point in getting milk. There were two or three unopened tins of dried in the cupboard. Eggs then. Eggs were always handy. Often Charlie liked fried eggs on his lunchtime rolls. He liked cakes too. She wrote eggs and cake down on the pad.

Standing chewing her pencil, Joel's face swam into her mind again. He had been in the Navy during the war. How odd that such vivid memories of him should insist on returning to her now. She could even feel the coarse texture of his navy-blue uniform and the

3

smoothness of the paler blue material that formed the square collar at the back. She remembered how his slimness was accentuated by the long, tight navy-blue top, and trousers that widened into bell-bottoms. For a few seconds she was warmed by the feel of serge and the heat of Joel's body glowing through it. She used to sit on his knee in her mother's front room. He'd put his arms around her and she'd lie against his chest with her head fitting perfectly into the curve of his neck. For hours they'd just sit like that — saying nothing, doing nothing. Yet it was the most wonderful feeling she'd ever had in her life. Just being with him.

Eventually her mother used to shout from the kitchenette, "Ann!"

When reluctantly she would separate herself from Joel's warm embrace and go through to the kitchenette her mother would say coldly, "It's time that man was out of here. It's nearly eleven o'clock at night."

Her mother had called him a man. Maybe because he was so tall — well over six feet. Poor Joel had been so self-conscious about his height he seldom could be persuaded to go to dances. He hated towering over everyone else and being conspicuous. Mostly they went to the cinema or for walks, or they just stayed at home. When he was on leave, that is. As often as not he was away at sea.

She decided to give the place a good hoovering and the flat was spick and span and the cushions plumped up by the time Charlie arrived.

"These roads get worse every day," he said. "There's more idiots driving cars in this city than anywhere else in the world."

Normally she would have let the remark pass without even noticing it but this time she immediately burst out with an emotional, "Don't be ridiculous!" She knew the heat of her response was uncalled for and she was surprised at herself. Charlie was obviously surprised too, and offended.

"You're a fine one to talk!" he retaliated.

He was referring to the car accident of some years back when she had been driving. She had never driven a car since. It gave her nightmares even to think about sitting behind a steering-wheel.

"That was a terrible thing to say, Charlie."

She prepared his lunch rolls and practically threw them at him. But Charlie had settled himself at the table and shut her out by opening his *Daily News*.

Eventually she said, "I wonder what they're doing now."

"Who?"

"Helen and Dave."

4

"What do you think they'll be doing? They're on their honeymoon, for God's sake." He was trying to appear as if he wasn't bothering about the busty nude on page three.

She sighed.

"There's no use going on like that," Charlie said. "She's a grown woman. A married woman now. You should have known you couldn't keep her a baby forever."

"Going on like what?"

"Giving tragic sighs."

"I wasn't sighing about her. I was sighing about you."

He laughed, making his ample belly heave. (Charlie had no time for "all this slimming nonsense".)

"I know you. You doted on that girl."

She watched his hand grope from beneath the *News* and slide one of his rolls out of sight. Sitting down opposite him she cut her roll in half then began chewing on it. Sometimes she tried to read a bit of the paper but Charlie moved it about too much.

"More tea?" she asked him.

"Eh?"

"Tea."

He flicked over page of the paper. "Are you having any?"

"Yes."

"I suppose I might as well."

She had a sudden urge to say something like, "Don't force yourself," or, "Don't do me any favours," or "Big deal!" But she controlled her tongue. After all, Charlie's remark had been harmless enough.

After the cups were filled Charlie blindly sugared his, leaving a white trail across the smoky glass table.

"Charlie!"

He smacked the paper down. "What's wrong with you now?"

"You're spilling sugar all over the table."

"Well, you've all day to wipe it up."

He cracked the *News* open again and she warmed her hands around her cup and watched his other rolls gradually disappear under the paper.

At last he let out a long belch.

"I wish you wouldn't do that," she told him.

Ignoring her, he eventually folded up his paper and glanced at his watch. Her eyes followed him as he fetched his jacket from behind the door and hitched it on. She always marvelled at his big drum of a chest. It gave him a peculiar kind of swagger, even when he stood still.

He planted his usual noisy kiss on her lips then said: "Cheer up. You'll soon be dead!"

5

For a long time after he went away she remained sitting at the table. The way her emotions kept heightening and sharpening was exhausting her. It was as much as she could do to stop herself from slithering over the glass top, head lolling on arms.

Impatient with her weakness she made a determined effort to rouse herself, collect her anorak and go out and get a breath of fresh air.

She passed her neighbour, Mrs Hennessy bustling backwards up the stairs, energetically bumping a pram. Baby Patrick's head was hitting the hood with monotonous regularity but he was far too busy concentrating on trying to hit the target of his mouth with a chocolate bar to notice this indignity.

"Hello, Mrs Sommerville," Mrs Hennessy panted. "Great weather for the ducks, eh?"

Still watching Patrick, Ann laughed. "He's enjoying that, isn't he? It doesn't seem so long ago that Helen was in her pram." Wistfulness deflated her laughter. "She had a wee white coat just like that."

"You'll miss her, Mrs Sommerville."

"Yes, the house isn't the same and East Dolton seems so far away. She's got a job in a shop out there to be nearer to her own place."

"Bus fares are murder, aren't they? I'd better get in. I haven't a bed made yet."

"I must rush too. 'Bye."

But as she emerged into Canal Lane and then crossed over into the busy Byres Road it occurred to her that there was no rush. Nothing urgent for her to do.

Then she remembered that there was a lecture in the Extra-Mural Department of the university. She'd seen it advertised in the library a few days previously. She decided she might as well go to that. She'd been to Zoë Middleton's lectures before and had enjoyed them, although the Shakespeare plays that Zoë read had never meant all that much to her.

She and Zoë had become quite friendly, and sometimes met for a coffee or a cup of tea in the Copper Kettle. Recently, however, Ann had noticed that Zoë was preferring something stronger, and on one occasion in fact had arrived on their doorstep drunk. Charlie had to take her home eventually. She thought she'd never hear the end of it from him, he went on about it so much even after Zoë had returned next day and apologized to him. Zoë was one of the nicest and most generous-natured of women when sober. But once she'd had a few gins she tended to get foul-mouthed. This was what shocked Charlie more than anything.

Today Ann discovered Zoë looking very *femme fatale* in a

'twenties-style black dress that glistened with jet beads at the neck and her blonde hair rippling over it like sunshine. Zoë was sharing the floor with a new lecturer called Simon Edgington and her eyes seemed drawn to him so flirtatiously and so often that she didn't notice Ann. At least she did not give her usual friendly greeting.

Edgington was a lean, cool, arrogant-looking man in his forties whose attitude to Zoë seemed more amused than encouraging. It was a distant sort of amusement as if he was pleased at Zoë's attentions yet had no desire to come within a mile of touching her. Loyalty to her friend made Ann dislike him at first. Then he read the sonnets with such poignancy that he riveted very different emotions on himself and on what he was saying. For the first time Shakespeare poetry was more to her than archaic language. It meant something in real human terms. She became filled to overflowing with admiration and appreciation for both author and tutor.

The discussion that followed the reading was mainly between the two lecturers, but Simon Edgington kept turning to the class and inviting their opinion and encouraging their reponse. His voice was patient and probing and he listened to everything that was said, no matter how inarticulate and halting, with what appeared genuine interest. Ann did not have the confidence to say anything but a couple of times, excited by a flare of understanding that unexpectedly illuminated her mind, words nearly tumbled out.

Returning to her empty flat she shivered, unsure if it was because she had so nearly risked making a fool of herself or because of the secret elation she was experiencing. Her emotions escaped and criss-crossed, weaving an illogical, contradictory pattern. She felt both excited and depressed, optimistic and apprehensive, thankful she'd gone to the class, and resentful of this new intrusion into her peace of mind, and she blamed Eric's unbearably loving letter for starting the ripple that was now spreading outwards and growing to dangerous proportions over the peaceful backwater of her life.

Chapter Two

"SOON BE time for good old Millport," Charlie rubbed his big hands together in anticipation.

Every year of their married life they'd gone to the small island of Millport for their annual holiday. She had never been wildly enthusiastic about the arrangement but had put up with it with good grace and been happy for Charlie's sake. He enjoyed it so much. She could always do what she fancied at other times during the summer, go away for a day or an afternoon to different places. Sometimes the Extra-Mural Department organized bus runs to places of historical or literary interest and she enjoyed those.

This year she didn't know how she could endure Millport. Twenty-five years of Millports ranged before her eyes, excruciating in their monotony.

"Why don't we go somewhere else for a change, Charlie?" she said. "There's so many other places to see. . . ."

Charlie chuckled and puffed contentedly at his pipe. "There's no place like good old Millport. You know you wouldn't be happy anywhere else."

It reminded her of every Saturday night when they went to the local pub. Even if one of the neighbours joined them and asked what she'd like to drink Charlie always interrupted with: "A pint of heavy for me and a sherry for her." If she said she'd prefer a gin and tonic or a dry Martini he scoffed at the mere idea.

"You *enjoy* sherry! It's *always* been your drink!"

Drink wasn't important to her and it never seemed worth making a fuss over. But at Millport she was denied the pleasure of reading. Charlie just wouldn't give her a minute's peace to read — unless of course while he was reading his paper. He stuck to her every minute of the day. He insisted on daily strolls with her, arm in arm along the front or through the Pleasure Gardens. He liked to look in shop windows with her pinioned to his side or relax with her, elbow to elbow, supping ice cream in cafés or glued to her at the local Pierrot Show where he kept guffawing and slapping her on the knee. Or they'd sit thigh to thigh on the sand and watch people frolicking about with beach balls. Charlie was a watcher, not a participator. As long as he had her by his side — "his other half", as he called her — he was perfectly content and happy.

For her to read in his company was an affront. It was as if she'd deserted him, or was punishing him for something. He couldn't bear in any way to be shut out or separate from her.

At first she had been flattered by this — what she'd thought of at the beginning of her marriage as intense love and devotion. After a childhood and young womanhood of seeing her mother's time and concern concentrated solely on her sister Constance, Charlie's attention had been a very welcome novelty and one which she'd enjoyed. She'd been grateful too. It was wonderful to feel needed and wanted and to belong to somebody.

Thinking back to her youth made her remember Joel again. She wondered what he looked like now. As tall and as handsome as ever, she was sure.

He had been a keen sportsman in his native Canada — an ice-hockey player, in fact. He must be middle-aged now. Were there

8

middle-aged ice-hockey players? She supposed not. Still, she couldn't imagine a man with such a splendid physique allowing it to go to seed. It had been so lean and firm. Broad shoulders tapered to a flat iron-hard belly, narrow hips and firm muscular thighs. Interesting that she should remember his physical appearance and her sensuous reactions to him so clearly. After all those years! Especially when they had never been physically intimate. In her day, and with her strict upbringing she wouldn't have dared commit what her mother would have regarded as an unforgiveable sin.

Charlie nudged her back to the present. "You're away in a dream."

"No, I wasn't."

"You're dreaming you're away on honeymoon with your kid."

"I wonder how they're getting on. I hope they'll be happy."

"Of course they'll be happy. Why shouldn't they be happy?"

She lit a cigarette and drew comfort from it before saying, "I hope she's picked the right one."

"Picked the right one?" Charlie always shouted when he was surprised. "I don't know what's come over you. Have you forgotten what her other guy *looked* like? He looked as if he had a headful of yellow horns. I've never seen such a freak. She's had a lucky escape, if you ask me. Picked the right one?" he roared. "The quicker you get away to Millport the better. You're going off your nut!"

Suddenly she felt like a kettle shooting to the boil. The scalding words, "Oh, shut up you loud-mouthed fool!" were only repressed in the nick of time. The rapidity of the effort needed to stifle herself, and the fact that she came within a hairbreadth of not succeeding, left her trembling. For a minute or two she couldn't grasp enough control to perform the simple movement of stretching her arm forward and lifting her cigarette. Eventually she managed it.

"What all these punks need," Charlie was saying now, "is a spell in the Army. First they'd get a bowl rammed over their nuts and a real short back and sides. Then they'd get a good sharp dose of discipline. They should bring back National Service. Nothing to beat it."

She blew out smoke and it drifted away with her attention. Despite Charlie's abrasive bawl she heard Simon Edgington's carefully modulated and cultured tones echoing around her like a haunting refrain.

"Thus have I had thee as a dream doth flatter,
In sleep a king, but waking no such matter. . . ."

All during that week at unexpected moments of the day and

9

sometimes at night when she couldn't sleep she would hear his voice, and his face would come unbidden and drift across her mind's eye. It was a closed, proud face, the grey eyes giving nothing away of the thoughts that lay behind them. They could unexpectedly soften, yet even then they seemed to have a concentrated force that tried to seek out the truth behind other people's faces. He was a disturbing man and she didn't want to see him again. But disappointment speared her when she discovered he was not at the next class. All the more so as it was the last class of the session. However, halfway through he did arrive and she experienced a rush of happiness and pleasure at the unexpected sight of him. The intensity of her emotion knocked her off-balance and brought on a hot flush. Embarrassed and confused, she lowered her head, pretending she was writing on her notepad and praying no one, especially Simon Edgington, would notice her foolishness.

After the class Zoë invited everyone up to her room in the university for a few glasses of wine, but before they all followed her and Simon away, she announced that Simon would be running a course of his own after the holidays.

Zoë kept Simon pretty much to herself after the preliminary gestures of hospitality had been met. She was a woman in her late thirties with a cupid's bow mouth and a starry sparkle to her eyes. Her eyes seemed continuously to talk volumes to Simon even when her mouth wasn't saying a word. At the same time she exuded relaxed and good-humoured friendship to everyone. She liked people and people knew it and were happy and at ease in her company even when she wasn't paying much attention to them. They helped themselves to Zoë's wine and perched up on her desk or lolled back against her bookshelves. A couple of the younger ones squatted down on the rug. Everyone chattered and laughed and became slightly tipsy. The wine was going to Ann's head too and detaching her in an absent-minded haze from the others. She kept arguing with herself about whether she should or shouldn't attend Simon's class after the holidays.

So obsessed and anxious was she in her secret conflict she didn't notice at first when everyone began filing out and saying their goodbyes. Startled to discover herself last in the room she hastened forward to shake hands with Simon but, unlike the others, could think of nothing to say to him. Lowering her head and blushing like a schoolgirl, she shrank timidly at his touch and when she did manage a smiling glance up at him she was further embarrassed by the glimmer of amusement she detected in his eyes.

She was furious with herself and called herself all the idiots under the sun on the way home. She had been tormented by hot

10

flushes for some time now, of course. Flashes would be a more appropriate word. So quickly and with such heat did they attack her. She had sought help from her doctor but he couldn't or wouldn't do anything to help.

"It's just your age," he said. "You'll be all right once you get a bit older."

When she'd been a young girl and suffering agonies with period pains the doctor had said she'd be all right once she got married. When she wasn't he'd said she'd be all right once she'd had a baby. Sometimes she felt very angry with doctors. Often she wished she was a man. This made Charlie furious.

"You don't know how lucky you are, that's your trouble. Because I'm a man I've to slave away on a treadmill to keep you, while all you do is loaf around and enjoy yourself."

She didn't envy Charlie's job on a car assembly line but often thought that he might have accepted that over the years she had done something to justify her existence even if it was only looking after him and sympathizing with him. She had given over a lot of her life to looking after Charlie and to keeping him company. Now she wished she hadn't devoted quite so much of her time to him.

She wished she'd been more outward-looking, done more interesting things, mixed with more interesting people so that she could have become more interesting herself. She even wished that she had not only read and enjoyed books but had studied them so that she could have been more articulate about them. Or at least have been able to make a few intelligent remarks to impress Simon Edgington instead of being struck dumb in his company.

She worried about what he must think of her all the way to Canal Lane. Then she felt depressed and even more foolish when it occurred to her that he probably wouldn't think of her at all. Why should he?

She bought a paperback copy of Shakespeare's *Sonnets* in The Thistle Bookshop, off Byres Road. But she didn't begin reading it until she'd finished *Lolita*. She liked to be tidy and organized, even with her reading habits. *Lolita* made her cry in the end and sonnets did nothing to cheer her up.

When forty winters shall besiege they brow,
And dig deep trenches in they beauties field. . . .

She put the book aside and sought comfort elsewhere.

Chapter Three

"MOTHER?"

There was the usual click at the other end of the telephone. Her mouth hardening, Ann replaced the receiver. She was not going to cry.

All right, she knew the accident had been a terrible shock to her mother. But it hadn't been her fault. A million times she'd told herself: *I did not kill my sister. It was not my fault.*

She and Constance had had their differences. Nevertheless she had loved her sister. Nights cuddling together in bed as children, whispers and giggles, and grandiose plans for the future rushed back to her.

Constance had been a pretty little girl two years younger than her. Had she been jealous of Constance's baby plumpness, her round blue eyes, her blonde curls and the innocent way she had of making everyone adore her? No, surely not. Many a battle she'd fought on her sister's behalf because although Constance had been doted on by grown-ups, children had not always nursed such generous feelings towards her, calling her things like "swot" and "teacher's pet". And because Constance was good at dancing as well as everything else, they bitterly taunted her with, "Think you're Shirley Temple? Well, you're not, see!"

Constance would come crying to her about these incidents and Ann would rush to punch the offender on the face, which did not exactly increase her own popularity rating. There had been a lot of offenders and a lot of punches, many of which had been most promptly and efficiently returned. Too many times she had arrived home bloodied and beaten, not to mention dirty and with torn clothes. Her mother, refusing to listen to any explanations, would invariably say, "I've just had about as much as I can take from you. Why can't you be more like Constance? You're nothing but a torment and a worry to me." And to anyone else who happened to be around she'd laugh and say, "One of these days that girl's going to drive me off my head. Did you ever see two such opposite children as my Constance and that girl? Queer, isn't it?"

Ann tried to be as clever as Constance at school. Looking back now she thought she'd probably tried too hard. In her desperation not only to pass each exam but to win a prize for being top in the class she flogged her nervous system and her brain to a standstill. Usually she ended up being sick or catching something filthy like chicken-pox just before the exams. . . .

But why was her mind drifting so much into the past? Now was the time, she told herself, for another visit to the new library.

12

It would have been quicker to have gone along Dumbarton Road to the old Partick Library but the new place was plushy with carpets and comfortable chairs to relax in. It also made a change of scenery to walk up Byres Road. She and Charlie never went shopping there. Charlie liked the cheaper shops in Partick.

But it wasn't just that. Byres Road and the area it led into was bed-sit land for hundreds of university students. There was the university itself and the many terrace houses and flats it had bought to house departments or members of staff.

"That Uni," said Charlie, "with all its long-haired layabouts, is taking over the whole of the city. That's what's wrong with the place."

Constance hadn't gone to university but she had got her "Highers" and then completed a teachers' training course.

Ann had been glad to leave school before then. She'd ended up working in a shop eventually but first she'd got a job pouring tea and peeling potatoes in a work's canteen.

Funnily enough, she'd met Joel in a canteen. There had been an Overseas Club in the city during the war and for some time after it. She had been one of the voluntary workers who cleared tables and washed dishes in the club in her spare time. She went with a girl-friend called Trudy who must be in her late forties now. She hadn't thought of Trudy for years. What a beautiful girl she'd been. A real gypsy type. If Trudy had wanted to, no doubt she could have charmed Joel away with one flap of her curly lashes.

Although, looking back, surely Joel had loved her? What had gone wrong then? Her mind strained to peer through the fog of a lifetime. She hadn't been too bad looking herself in those days with her warm brown hair and eyes, and long lashes. And she'd had a nice slim figure.

Her mother had regarded Joel as another of her disasters, of course.

"Trust you," she groaned, "to pick a Catholic. And your Dad and I life-long and well respected members of the Masons and the Star."

"I don't care about religion," she'd protested.

"And your grandpa would turn in his grave if he knew," her mother had continued. "He was a Grand Master. Dear knows where you might end up or what trouble you might land yourself in."

Her mother needn't have worried. She had been too shy and touchy to grab her chance when it came. Joel had been cradling her on his knee the night before he'd gone back to his ship — the last time Ann was ever to see him or touch him — and she'd eventually murmured, "What are you thinking?"

13

He had replied, "I'm thinking about jewellery stores and rings, honey."

For some crazy reason she found it hard to understand even now, she had tensed up and snapped back, "Oh? Why?"

And he had sighed.

How she remembered that sigh now. For the first time she heard the hopelessness in it. She had been hardly more than a child and painfully shy and uncertain of herself. Only now, a lifetime later, she realized that he, a boy of nineteen, had been equally shy and unsure of himself.

"It doesn't matter," he'd said retreating, not into the blissful silence that had united them before but far away into unhappy aloneness.

His sigh echoed down through the years. All those years and she could still hurt with love for him. Who would have thought it? This realization brought back worries about Helen and Eric.

She remembered how Helen, when telling her about the last quarrel with Eric, had burst out tragically: "It's all over, Mum!"

"You'll fall in love again," she'd soothed. "First love's just a part of growing up. Believe me, Helen, you'll get over it and you'll even be glad eventually."

"No, I'll never stop loving Eric," Helen had sobbed broken-heartedly. "I'll love him for the rest of my life."

Hardly aware of the title Ann took a book to the desk then returned outside.

A breeze was making open umbrellas of Laura Ashley skirts, sticking T-shirts and denims to youthful bodies and lifting long hair to swirl it gaily around. Because of the university there were always more young people than old to be seen.

She had a look at the shops, especially the Indian shops and the boutiques that had music playing all the time and so many fascinating odds and ends, jewellery and pottery and basketwork and jars of herbs and spices as well as trendy clothes. Then there were the delicatessens. On an impulse she went into one and pointed at one of the dishes on display.

"What's that?"

"Moussaka."

"It looks interesting."

"It's very nice."

"I'll try some."

She bought a tin of green figs as well, and some intriguing pink cheese. The brown bread seemed so fresh and crusty she couldn't resist a loaf. It would be a change from her usual sliced white. She was quite looking forward to the meal by the time she got home, and a taste of the moussaka while she was dishing it made her close

14

her eyes and moan to herself with appreciation. It was delicious.

"What's this mess?" Charlie said, staring in astonishment and disbelief at his plate.

"Moussaka, they call it. I got it in the delicatessen up Byres Road. I don't know what they put in it but. . . ."

"I don't know what they put in it either and I don't want to know!"

". . . it has such a different, delicate kind of flavour. Try it, Charlie. Oh, go on, please!" She felt excited. Her emotions seemed to have gone haywire. They were so easily roused.

He prodded it with his fork as if examining it for bugs. Then he took a forkful, chewing with a contorted face and screwed up nose. She had never seen him look so ugly.

Her excitement fizzled out, leaving her sad and bitter. "Don't force yourself. I'll make something else."

"No," he sighed. "I'll eat the stuff rather than waste it."

She tried not to watch him. She produced the pink cheese and the figs but Charlie was so outraged by them that she was forced to go through to the kitchen and open a tin of creamed rice. Automatically she added lots of sugar — Charlie had a terrible sweet tooth — and heated it while he was watching "Ivor the Engine" on television.

Later there was a war film and she tried to read a book instead of watching it. But as usual, Charlie wouldn't leave her in peace.

"You're missing a good picture."

"We've seen it before."

"So what? So we know it's a good picture."

She took her book through to the kitchen and hunched with it over the glass table. The seat was hard and the room cold and soon Charlie was at her elbow coughing pipe smoke down on her head and saying,

"What's come over you? How long are you going to make my life a misery like this?"

"For goodness sake, Charlie, I'm only trying to read a book."

"I know you. You're making me sit through there by myself as some sort of punishment. Well, let's get this straight once and for all. It wasn't my fault some man stole your kid."

"I said, I'm only trying to read a book."

"You've all day to read books."

She couldn't deny this. It had also to be admitted to herself that although it hadn't been her intention to punish Charlie by coming through to the kitchen, she could see that it was a punishment. Charlie didn't like to be on his own. That didn't mean that he was sociable. Far from encouraging her to invite friends to the house he made it so difficult she seldom bothered.

15

She had never thought of it for years but now she realized how in the first flush of happiness and hope in her marriage she had been full of plans — entertaining friends, moving house, changing furniture around, adventuring into new and strange places on holiday. But Charlie, she had discovered, didn't like adventuring. He was a family man, he said. He liked his wife to be there all the time, at his side, where she should be. Literally at his side. All the time.

Closing her book and rising from the kitchen table, she tried to tell herself that she was lucky. Yet when she and Charlie settled side by side on the settee facing the television and Charlie patted her hand she felt irritated beyond measure. It was as if he'd said, "Good dog!" Even his contentment irritated her. And he was contented and happy with his attention glued to the screen and her, as usual, beside him. His "other half".

Her eyes slide round to study him. A lifetime they'd been married. It seemed incredible. The way he sucked at his pipe, slowly, contentedly, began to really screw up her nerves. She had to look away before the urge to ram the pipe down his throat completely overcame her.

Chapter Four

"WE WON'T come over next Sunday, Mum, because we're having some friends for a meal. And during the week's no use. By the time Dave and I get home from work and have our dinner and get organized for the next day. . . . But maybe the following Sunday. I'll give you a ring, anyway."

They were saying their goodbyes at the door and Ann kissed Helen again. She longed to say, "But I could come over and see you any night during the week. I don't care about the long bus run or being late getting back."

But in case Helen didn't want her to come, and trying not to appear hurt, all she said was, "All right, love. Safe journey home."

It seemed unreal to think that "home" to Helen was no longer here but an anonymous high-rise flat in East Doltan. She still could not convince herself that it was true.

"Well," said Charlie after the door was shut, "now that you've seen she's all right, you can stop your worrying."

But Ann was running through to the front room to wave from the window and to continue waving until Dave's car disappeared from sight.

Then a strange thing happened. The pang she felt at losing Helen somehow became mixed with Simon Edgington and she experienced such a longing for him it was as if he had been the one she'd known and loved for a lifetime and they'd just said goodbye.

Shaken, she went through to the bedroom, undressed, slid between the sheets and closed her eyes. She and Charlie had separate beds and she always left his bedlight on to guide him safely into the room. Tonight she turned away from it into the darkness, clutching the sheets up to her mouth, clinging to them as if to protect herself from the quicksands that were shifting dangerously around her. Her mind retreated again to the old woman at the other end of the city who had once been the rock in her life, strong in body and will, dependable, never-changing. Seventy-six her mother was now and as bitter and unforgiving as the day of the accident.

Now her imagination had shifted once more.

She was in Charlie's car and she was driving. Her sister Constance was sitting beside her. She was chatting to Constance but as usual Constance didn't appear to be listening. Then from a side street without any warning, another car shoots out. Her sister screams. Her chattering stops. Her stomach hardens. Her foot stamps on the brake. Tyres dig into the road. Then losing their grip on the wet slippery surface, the car accelerates faster. The two cars come together with a shuddering impact. Everything is in slow motion. The wing mirror shatters and sails slowly away. The wing crumples and curls up round the bonnet. The front rearside wheel wrenches from the hub and bounces in gigantic leaps down the road. The steering-wheel spins loose in her hands. The car slews round and floats across the carriageway. She sees a lorry. The driver's face is stiff with horror. The articulated trailer swings towards the car like a giant crocodile's tail and crushes it into darkness.

A coffin between chairs. Wax faces of the living as well as the dead.

Mother saying, "Why did it have to be you who survived? Constance had so much to offer life, so many worthwhile things to give."

Explanations made no difference to her mother's attitude, either about the accident itself or how, in the first place, Constance's car had broken down and she had phoned and asked to be picked up.

"Constance asked me, Mother. She was stranded. I was trying to help."

"I'll never forgive you," her mother kept repeating. "I don't want anything more to do with you."

The lorry driver and all the other witnesses swore it wasn't her fault. The driver of the other car admitted full responsibility. There was nothing she could do. Everyone said so. But afterwards she had gone to her mother's house and the door was slammed in her face. She had tried to speak to her in the street and been ignored. Letters had been returned. Desperate words were flung into silence before the cut-off click of the phone at the other end.

Had she been talking too much that day in the car? Had her concentration been one hundred per cent perfect? Charlie had never wanted her to learn to drive and always insisted she would never be any use at it. Was there anything else she could have, should have done that day of the accident?

Opening her eyes wide, she strained to see through a wet blur and was startled by Charlie's voice, "All the tears in the world aren't going to bring your kid back."

She looked round at him. He was zipping down his trousers.

"So there's no use just lying there feeling sorry for yourself," he said. "Move over. I'll soon cheer you up."

She wiped her eyes on the sheet. She knew he would not immediately come to bed. He would go into the same routine he had been acting out for the whole of their married life. Charlie had got into the habit of folding an old towel underneath her backside as if he was going to work on his car. Then he lubricated her with Vaseline.

Nothing was less romantic than Charlie padding away to fetch the towel and the tin of Vaseline wearing nothing but his aertex vest. He never wore pyjamas except on holidays. She tried not to look. Her mind beat about seeking escape but found none. Until at long, long last Charlie left her and climbed into his own bed.

"Goodnight."

"Goodnight, dear," she said.

She knew he was disappointed. She had not even been able to simulate enjoyment.

Charlie was still a bit huffy with her next morning. He didn't come into the bedroom and give her a kiss or say cheerio. Even at lunchtime she detected a certain coolness emanating from behind the *Daily News*.

"There's a good Western on telly tonight," she said, in an effort to make up for her own deficiencies. Charlie liked Westerns.

A reluctant "Oh?" issued from behind the paper.

"With John Wayne," she encouraged.

She felt the thaw as he turned the pages. He didn't say anything but his hand was more relaxed as it groped over his plate.

After the last salad roll had disappeared she listened to his munching contentedly for a while then said, "Charlie, would you like me to get up earlier and see to your breakfast?"

Surprised, he lowered the paper. "Why?"

"Well, it would save you the bother. I mean, while you're

shaving I could be doing your eggs or sausages or whatever you fancy. . . ."

"You know I don't like anybody in my way in the mornings. Even before I was married I always put myself out to work. You know that."

"Yes, but. . . ."

"Well, why are you coming out with such a daft idea?"

"Well, I just thought. . . . Oh, never mind."

Rolling his eyes, he disappeared behind his paper again.

She sipped her tea and fell to wondering how she'd spend the afternoon. She was too restless, her emotions were too over-stimulated to settle to read. Perhaps she could walk along to the Kelvin Hall. The exercise would do her good.

"What's on in the Kelvin Hall?" she asked Charlie as he was going for his jacket.

"The carnival's finished."

"I'm not bothered about the carnival. That was all right when Helen was small. Remember how she loved it?"

"You mean *you're* going?"

"Is there any reason I shouldn't? I've done the housework, and tonight's dinner's all prepared."

"By God! Some people have a right cushy number."

"I do my work."

"Work?" Charlie's laughter was good-humoured.

"Yes, work," she replied, her eyes hardening, challenging.

When she thought of the times, long before she'd acquired any labour-saving gadgets — the times she used to rub for hours at an old washboard then struggle to turn the handle of the wringer until her back was about broken, the times she'd been down on her knees scrubbing floors, the times she'd thrashed about with a carpet beater — and what about all the cooking and sewing she'd done, not to mention nursing when Charlie or Helen had been ill.

Charlie laughed again. "Have a good time. And just you remember how lucky you are. While you're enjoying yourself strolling around the Kelvin Hall I'll be slaving my guts out."

The words "Drop dead!" burned red hot in her skull but before she could say them Charlie had gone. To add to her irritation, she dropped a cup while clearing the table. "Damn!"

She washed the rest and as quickly as she could set the gateleg table in the front room ready for the evening meal. Then she collected her shopper and handbag and set off.

It wasn't until she was away along Dumbarton Road that it occurred to her she didn't need her shopper. Yet the mere idea of being without it made her feel strangely insecure. When Helen had been small it had been absolutely essential to carry spare nappies

19

and bottles and bibs and rusks and teddies. Now that she came to think of it, carrying a shopper had become a habit — a kind of identity badge of wife and mother.

The large red sandstone building that housed the circus and carnival over the Christmas season, and events like the Motor Show and the Modern Homes Exhibition at other times of the year, loomed ahead. Suddenly she was reminded of hundreds of other visits to the Kelvin Hall and how exhausting they had been. That was, she realized, all she did remember about them: the endless trailing around among crowds of people and getting more and more tired.

Charlie love the huge hall. He always treated Helen and her to an ice-cream cone and they wandered about licking and looking. Helen had enjoyed these outings as much as Charlie.

"Look at that, Dad! Look at this, Dad!" She'd tug him this way and that. Or she'd hang happily on to his arm.

Ann stopped at the door. Already she could hear the loud, hollow echoes of the place. She did not need to go in. The thought made her feel unexpectedly cheerful. The Art Galleries and Museum across the road caught her eye and she decided on impulse that she would go there instead. It would be a change. She hadn't been for years.

She remembered her father taking her when she was a child. He had been a quiet man whose time was mostly taken up with work and the Masons and of course he'd died when she was a teenager. But before that there had been occasions when he'd taken her to the Art Galleries and she'd enjoyed looking at the pictures.

As she entered the building now, the first thing she noticed was the open-plan coffee-bar in the middle of the display area on the ground floor. That was an innovation. She stood admiring the bright colour and pleasing design of tables and chairs. After she had a walk around she'd treat herself to a coffee. She relished the prospect in her mind — as if she'd never had a cup of coffee in her life before.

Upstairs, the first picture that caught her attention was hung at the end of a long corridor. She recognized it as Dali's painting of Christ of St John of the Cross. There had been a photograph in a newspaper and a bit of publicity about it when the council had bought the painting several years ago. This, however, was the first time she had set eyes on the real thing.

She stood for a long time staring at it from the distance of the corridor. At first she was unable to sort out her emotions and make sense of them. Pleasure, pity, admiration, sorrow, a disintegration into secret tears, awe and reverence made a confusion of her feelings. She kept thinking in amazement that the man who had

20

painted this was the same man that the newspapers had made seem so crazy and ridiculous.

Charlie had been outraged that so much public money had been "tossed down the drain".

"They obviously think it's smart to pander to cranks and madmen, but I don't. I could never earn that amount of money slaving for the rest of my life. I know what I'd do with Dali and the local government men who bought his picture. Put them up against the nearest wall and shoot the lot of them."

Gladness that by the merest chance she had wandered into this place soothed and relaxed her.

Strolling towards the painting she savoured every moment. She examined it close up and from this angle and that. Then she proceeded to explore the various rooms that led off the corridor. There was too much to see and respond to. Overwhelmed, she sat down on a bench in the centre of one of the rooms. She sat tidily with feet together and back straight. She tucked her hair neatly behind her ear. With her handbag and shopper perched on her lap she remained for a long time her large brown eyes staring at a picture on the wall opposite. It was called "Hesperus, the evening star sacred to lovers", and it seemed to have captured such delicate love and tenderness.

Ann could have remained there all day devouring it with her eyes.

Chapter Five

SHE COULD hardly wait to tell Charlie. On wings of excitement she flew along the lobby the moment she heard his key in the door.

"Charlie, I had a great time this afternoon. . . ."

"Let me get in and get my jacket off. Some of us have done a hard day's work, you know."

"I just wanted to tell you. . . ."

"Yes, all right, but it'll surely keep until I go to the bathroom."

He disappeared, leaving her staring at the frosted-glass panel of the bathroom door.

By the time he emerged again she had made a pot of tea, dished the chips, arranged fresh fruit salad in a glass bowl and was waiting impatiently on the edge of her chair.

Charlie went over and switched on the television. Then, backing away from the set as if afraid it might disappear, his bottom groped for his chair and without dragging his attention from the screen, his hands found the cutlery at either side of his plate.

"Magic Roundabout" was on.

21

"Well? Hurry up! It'll soon be the news," said Charlie.

"Hurry up with what?"

"Tell me about your great time at the Kelvin Hall."

Much of her eagerness had gone flat but she managed to retain some lift to her voice. "Oh, I didn't go there."

For the first time Charlie looked at her. "Didn't go to the Kelvin Hall?"

"I went across to the Art Galleries instead."

"What on earth for?"

"A change, I suppose."

"The change of life. That's what's up with you." He sighed. "It's terrible what men have to suffer."

"Men? Men have to suffer? That's a laugh. Sometimes you're priceless, Charlie. Absolutely priceless!"

"Stands to reason. When women go queer they take it out on their men. They make the men suffer."

"I'm not going queer."

"I don't think much of your pies. Have you been going to that delicatessen again?"

"They taste lovely to me."

"I knew it." Sadly, he pushed his plate away.

"For goodness' sake, Charlie!"

"For years you've bought perfectly good pies from Leitches, the butcher."

"For years. And years. *And* years!"

"What's up with you now?"

"Oh, shut up!"

"Charming! Oh, charming, I must say."

She forced herself to go on chewing and swallowing. "There's nothing wrong with these pies."

"You'd say that if it choked you."

She watched him make a martyr of himself by touching nothing but his bread and butter. She tried not to feel guilty but failed.

With much bitterness Charlie said, "Had a good time, did you?"

His face was squarish with heavy jowls. He kept his wiry grey hair cropped short, despite being teased by Helen about it making him look like an ancient punk rocker. He was needing a shave and the bristle on his jowls was a sicklier shade than his head, more white than grey.

"Until I came back here," she said.

"Oh, I'm sorry I can't keep you entertained when I come in from doing a hard day's work."

"Charlie, the way you go on, you'd think no one ever did a stroke of work but you."

"A couple of days on that assembly line would kill you. You

22

don't know you're born. You're making me miss the news!"
Suddenly aware of the announcer's voice he hooked his eyes on to
the screen. Then without dividing his attention he managed to
squash some chips between two slices of bread and wolf them
down.

Automatically she finished her pie then dished the fruit salad.
Nothing more was said for three hours. Suddenly she became
aware that Charlie had bustled up from his seat.

"We've half an hour before the film comes on the other side. I'll
help you with the dishes."

With an effort she gathered the dishes together and stacked them
on the tray.

Charlie said, "I'll go and boil a kettle of water." Then once they
were both through at the sink, "Well, then? What was there at the
Art Galleries to get all worked up about?"

Dish-washing time was talking time.

She shrugged nonchalantly. Yet a spark of enthusiasm rekindled
as she remembered.

"There were some lovely pictures. Remember that Dali one we
read about in the papers? You should have seen it, Charlie. It's
really got something. You seem to be looking down at Jesus from a
great height. A kind of God's-eye view. And although you can't see
the expression on Christ's face, even the top of his head seems to
speak volumes."

"That's daft."

Charlie's back looked embarrassed and she became infected by
his discomfort. Blushing as if she'd said something that ought to be
apologized for, she loudened her voice.

"No, honestly, Charlie."

"He's a fruit and nut case."

"Who?"

"It's all very well for folk like that. They've got nothing better to
do."

"Dali, you mean?"

"Some of these guys would do anything for money. It's like these
pop stars. It's all a publicity stunt. A big con. Bing Crosby or
Richard Tauber had more talent in their little fingers than all of
these crazy guys put together."

"Whether Dali's crazy or not makes no difference."

"I bet it makes a difference to his wife. God knows what she's
had to suffer."

"To his painting, I mean. That picture was really good."

"What do you know about painting? You wouldn't know one end
of a paint brush from the other. If you're so keen on painting why
is it I'm always the one that's to do the woodwork in here? And

23

outside. Just look at these ledges already."

"How can you compare window-ledges with a painting by Dali?"

"You're right, there's no comparison. We need window-ledges. Window-ledges are of some use to folk."

"Dali has. . . ."

"I know what Dali has. A head full of maggots."

"Charlie!"

"Pay attention!"

"What?"

"You haven't washed the cutlery yet. The film will be on in a minute. It's John Wayne remember."

"Right!" said Charlie, after they'd returned to the sitting-room. Tossing a miniature bottle of sherry on her lap he added, "Don't say I'm not good to you."

He opened his can of beer and filled his dimpled glass mug with proud concentration, at the same time as his big square bottom dug a more comfortable position on the settee.

Sitting beside him she marvelled at the increasing conflict of her emotions. All of a sudden she couldn't bear Charlie. More and more she longed to say something bitter and nasty to him. Surely this must be unfair? Guilty and ashamed she attempted to make amends by moving closer to him and giving his arm an affectionate squeeze. Still utterly absorbed with the television his horny fingers fastened over her thigh laying claim to her. With his other hand, he took a swig of beer.

Later, when it was time for their mugs of tea and cakes (Charlie looked forward to a jam doughnut or a cream sponge at night), he noticed that something was wrong.

"What's up?"

"Nothing."

"What are you looking so miserable for, then?"

She avoided his eyes. "I've a terrible headache, Charlie."

"You sit there then. I'll make the tea and bring it through."

Her mouth twitched in a wretched smile of thanks.

Even when Charlie was being kind she couldn't bear him. Maybe he was right and it was the change of life; that, and finding Eric's letters and Helen leaving. Even in some strange way the new tutor at the extra-mural class. She had seen, as well as the amusement in Simon Edgington's eyes, a faint glimmer of interest when he'd looked at her. It made her desperate to be worthy of that interest. Like the way at school she used to work like a creature possessed at her lessons if a teacher smiled at her or said a kind word. She had been so young and eager and full of hope then. Now she was just a dull middle-aged housewife tied to boring household routines. But, damn it, why should she be tied? What was to prevent her even going out to work if she wanted to? Why shoudn't she seek new interests and challenges? You can only be an interesting person if you lead a full and interesting life.

Totally oblivious to the John Wayne film now going full guns on the television she allowed her mind to follow this path, getting more and more excited as she did so.

She waited until she was in bed before she broached the subject in a burst of enthusiasm.

"I know what I need, Charlie."

He gave a coarse, sandpaper laugh. "You can never get enough of it can you?"

"Charlie!"

"Not tonight, Josephine!"

She tutted impatiently at him. "What I need is a job."

Charlie's eyes bulged with indignation. "You've got a job. Looking after me. That's your job."

"An outside job I mean. Something to give me an interest."

"What do you want? Jam on it? I've provided you with a good house and every labour-saving gadget, and a twenty-two-inch coloured telly and I take you out twice a week to the pub. What more can I do?"

"I'm not asking you to do any more."

"You're saying that I haven't done enough."

"I am not."

"That I'm not able to keep you."

"Nothing of the kind."

"It's an insult!"

"How old-fashioned can you get?"

"Oh, charming! I'm old-fashioned as well!"

"All I meant was that nobody thinks anything about women going out to work now. Look at Helen. She's married, and she's working."

"I don't want to know about other men's wives. I've enough on my plate trying to cope with my own."

"I don't see what you're complaining about."

"It's you that's complaining."

"For pity's sake! All I'm saying is that I'm at a loose end for most of the day and it's a bit depressing. I just thought it might be a good idea to try to find something interesting to do, something stimulating, something to occupy my mind, Charlie."

"What's wrong with the Bingo? All the other women go there in the afternoons."

"I can't play for a start."

"That's because you've never been. The others would show you.

You're surely not that daft."

"No, but. . . . ."

"You just haven't a clue what to be at since Helen left the house except to keep going on at me. You'd never do for a job anyway. You're far too dreamy."

"I'm shy, that's all. I feel awkward in company when you're not there. That's why I don't fancy going to the Bingo."

He looked slightly mollified at that. But his voice retained its abrasive accusing tone.

"You've known everyone around here for donkey's years. What's there to be shy about? You're just being stupid."

"No, I'd rather be on my own."

"You were blethering about going out to work a minute ago."

"That's different."

"If you were serving in a shop you'd be among strangers."

"Yes, but I'd have a particular role to play. I mean, I'd know what to do and say."

Charlie looked miserable as he thumped into bed. "You get on my wick. Just shut up and go to sleep."

She felt miserable herself now.

"Goodnight, Charlie."

He turned his back on her and she barely heard his muffled reply. She clung to the idea of a job though. Now that she thought of it, there had been a postcard in the window of one of the boutiques in Byres Road advertising for a shop assistant. It would be most interesting to work there and she had plenty of shop experience and good references. She imagined herself among all the racks of trendy clothes, and boxes of Eastern jewellery, and baskets of coloured tights, and shawls, and cotton, and shelves of pottery, and jars of spices and herbs. . . . There was lots of fun as well as interest in working in a shop, the variety of different types of customer, the giggled confidences between the assistants about their social life of the night before.

It would take her out of herself. That was all she needed.

Chapter Six

THE FIRST thing she did the next morning after Charlie left for work was to put on the immersion heater. Then, as soon as the water was heated, she had a bath and dressed in the brown suit and beige silk blouse she'd worn at Helen's wedding. A dab of rouge, some bright lipstick, a hint of eye make-up accentuated the radiant glow of her face. *Today*, she kept thinking, *I'm starting a new life*.

Sunshine welcomed her outside, and as she walked briskly up

Byres Road she found extra pleasure in catching glimpses of her reflection in shop windows. Its smartness excited her. Even her short hair had an unusual gloss and bounce to it. Happiness lent wings to her heels and carried her swiftly to the door of the boutique.

There was no counter, but at the far end of the shelf, along one side of the tube-like premises, a cash register could barely be seen among a sparkling gold and silver display of lurex tights. Also beside the till was a mountain of grey mugs on which were painted in blood red: "Drink to me only", "You're the dregs", and "Hiya Sugar". Three assistants, two female and one male, lounged gossiping together in the corner. It was too early for the shop to be busy and they all stared round in surprise when she walked up to them.

"I'd like to see the manageress, please."

"I'm the manageress," said one of the gossipers, a wariness creeping round the edges of her voice.

"Could I speak to you for a minute, please?"

"Yes." The manageress did not detach herself from the group even when Ann glanced at the others in some embarrassment.

"It was about your advert."

"Advert?" Surprised eyes swivelled round at her colleagues. "We didn't advertise any stock this week, did we?"

"Oh, no," Ann said. "The advert in the window about a job."

"You know somebody who's interested?"

"Well, actually," she smiled, "it's me. I'd like to apply."

The manageress registered no emotion but Ann suspected that her wide-eyed blank look was a cover for hilarity. Faced with this over-stretched stare she suddenly became confused and anxious.

"I've excellent references." Lowering her head she began fumbling in her handbag, at the same time sensing glances were being exchanged between the others. At last she found the references and handed them over. "I was with Coppard's for most of the time."

"Coppard's? Where's that? I've never heard of it."

"Oh, it's . . . it's knocked down now."

It occurred to her that the manageress was as young as, if not younger than, her own daughter. The assistants were even more youthful. The boy had a fiery rash of spots on a pasty face and wore a black T-shirt over baggy trousers that tightened in at his ankles. The girl had a stringy mop of hair and wore brown rouge and lipstick and a black mini-dress like a sack tied low down on her hips and flounced out in two layers of scarlet-edged frills.

"It was in the city centre — a very high-class shop. I was well trained there. I know how to look after stock as well as customers."

27

The girl tittered, and from the corner of her eye Ann saw the boy nudge her. She tried to tell herself that young people just giggled for the sake of giggling. They didn't mean any harm.

"I'm a very conscientious worker. It tells you there," she indicated one of the references.

The manageress clung fixedly to her unblinking stare. She had enormous false lashes, spiking like stars from plum-painted lids.

"It was really somebody younger I was looking for."

"Oh, I see." Ann accepted the return of her references and tucked them neatly into her handbag. Then she lingered as if hopefully expecting the manageress to say something else. When nothing else came she attempted a smile.

"Well, never mind. No harm done. It's a lovely day, isn't it? Summer's come at last. We'll get a suntan yet."

Clumsily picking her way between the baskets of T-shirts and tights, she somehow reached the door. She couldn't face going back to the house and made for the Light Bite snack bar instead.

The cup was thick and the tea slopped over into the saucer but she didn't care. Finding a seat by herself over at the window she sipped the bitter brew and stared out at people passing in Byres Road.

Unable to give up the idea of a job, she thought that perhaps she had just chosen the wrong place. Rather than a suburban boutique maybe it would be more sensible to try one of the big stores in the centre of town. There had been an advertisement in the paper for assistants. Her optimism returned. As soon as she had finished her tea she would hop on a bus and try the store that had advertised.

It was while she was waiting for a bus that she saw Simon Edgington. He seemed to stand out from the busy throng of people in Byres Road. He was so startlingly handsome and distinguished looking and so elegantly dressed he made everyone else, in Ann's eyes at least, look shabby and uniformly dull. He wore a beige safari suit so immaculate it could have been brand new. Its light colour emphasized his tanned skin and dark hair, and eyes that were clouded with thought.

A bus came and Ann propelled herself hurriedly on to it although the effort needed surprised her. Her legs seemed boneless and her heart had a fast, feeble beat, yet it resounded all over her body. She tried to tell herself not to be foolish. A woman of her age! And as if to accentuate her age she felt a hot flush that brought beads of sweat to trickle down between her breasts. The bus transported her safely away from Byres Road but she was still being consumed with heat. Even her hair felt hot and clammy and, as soon as she reached town and alighted, she ran her fingers through it and tossed her head back and took several deep breaths of cooling air.

She felt harassed and insecure just when she needed to be cool and confident for the interview. It irritated her. Was she going to have to hide indoors all the time in case she met Simon Edgington and behaved, for all to see, like a silly blushing schoolgirl? She vowed that next time she went to the doctor she would *insist* on being given something to calm her wayward emotions.

Most of Sauchiehall Street in the city centre was now a pedestrian precinct with plants and flowers in barrels and benches to sit on. One seat was occupied by a couple of unshaved winos sleeping propped against one another, loose-mouthed and limbed like a couple of dirty rag dolls. On another seat a gaggle of giggly young people were sharing secrets with their potato chips.

Ann crossed the road past the busker in the tartan cap and trousers who was jauntily playing the flute. On reaching the store that had advertised she pushed her way through the swing doors. The ground floor was a maze of racks hung with crushed blouses and cotton skirts and denims. Girls, as fresh as morning dew with long shimmering hair and sparkling eyes, were searching about, jerking hangers off rails and holding garments up for inspection.

It had never been like that in her day. If you wanted to buy a dress you went to a shop and an assistant immediately came forward to attend to your needs. Times without number she had approached customers with an encouraging smile and a deferential, "Can I help you, Madam?" The next step was to lead the customer to a fitting-room and after securing "Madam's" privacy by drawing the velvet curtain she would proceed to the rail of gowns in the showroom. This rail extended the whole length of the oak wall and was protected by glass doors with brass locks. From this hallowed cupboard she selected a few garments which she took to the fitting-room.

In her day, shop assistants had worn black dresses. The manageress had also worn black but she was distinguished by a pearl necklace. Now it was not only impossible to differentiate between manageress and assistants but between assistants and customers.

Could that be an assistant in skin-tight blue jeans and what appeared to be an outsize khaki army shirt gathered somewhere lower than the middle by a silver-buckled belt? Could that be the manageress with the glossy lips and pink hair frizzed and standing on end? Or could she be that blonde wearing the top like a Victorian granny's chemise and a skirt like the same granny's petticoat?

Ann's gaze and fingers raked her bag to make sure her references were still safe. Then, tucking a stray lock of hair back behind her ear, she smiled and edged along between the racks to where the girl

29

in the granny clothes was standing filing her nails.

"Could I speak to the manageress, please?"

Without a word and still attending to her nails the girls sauntered over to one of the racks. There, a young woman whom Ann had not noticed before was examining blouses. Unashamedly plump in a dress and trousers in scarlet and with black hair cut short and fringed, the woman bore down on her.

"You wanted to speak to me?" She had a kindly smile that lit a fire of gratitude in Ann's heart.

"It was about the job you have advertised. I would like to apply. I haven't worked for quite a few years but I know I could do it," she rushed hopefully on. "I was always very conscientious. I realize that stock and fashions have changed, but anyone can soon learn what the stock is, and where it is. The *important* thing is to realize that the customer comes first and to treat every customer with politeness and interest and to attend to their requirements as conscientiously as possible." The pity melting the manageress's eyes made Ann confused and anxious again. "Don't you think?" she ended lamely.

"Actually, I've just engaged a girl. I'm sorry. Why don't you try an older store? Maybe something local." The plump face melted with concern. "I'm sure you'll find something."

"Yes, of course. You've a very nice shop here. Very bright and cheerful."

As she left, Ann bumped into a clothes rack, said an automatic "Sorry," then laughed again. Outside, she walked along without knowing where she was going. She kept thinking, *It's all different now. It's a different world. I'm out of touch.*

It seemed incredible. The Central Reference Library caught her her eye and, seeking a quiet refuge she made for the large domed building. Inside, at a sea of desks in the main hall, students bent over books. Some were diligently filling sheaves of paper with notes. They all looked so young, they made her want to cry. She had to retreat out to the street again. Eventually she found a bus that carried her home.

Just in time, she had the rolls spread for Charlie's lunch.

He didn't speak all through the meal. No more than a few words were exchanged at the best of times. This morning, however, she had told Charlie she was going after a job and he was in a huff with her. He only ate one roll, leaving the other two on his plate as a constant reminder of how she was making him suffer. She wanted to tell him about her humiliation so that she could draw closer to him for comfort and understanding, although this was a mirage that seldom if ever materialized. And because of that she was instinctively afraid to begin. Forced on by her need, however, she at last confessed to the headlines of the *Daily News*.

"I didn't get the job."

Immediately Charlie put down the paper. "I knew you wouldn't get it. I told you you wouldn't get it. I told you it was a waste of time."

"Nobody would ever get anywhere if they didn't try."

"What happened?"

To speak of her morning's experience was like peeling the protective dressing from a wound. Her face creased with anxiety as she related the events. Afterwards, Charlie guffawed.

"Never mind, old wife, I'll be retiring soon and I'll be here all day to keep you company. We'll be a real old Darby and Joan together."

He wolfed down the other two rolls, finished reading his paper, then, whistling absentmindedly, he collected his jacket.

"I'm away," he said, kissing her. "Cheer up, you'll soon be dead!"

It was as if Charlie's kiss was the kiss of death. She did not move or think after he left. She neither knew nor cared how long she remained in this comatose state. Until, through the sterile blue and white silence of the kitchen, she became aware of the panicky ticking of her watch. It seemed to scatter her wits. She had to move. She had to do something. But she didn't know what to do. Out of habit she got up to clear the table. At the same time, the knowledge that her reaction was automatic brought even more paralysing confusion. She fumbled, knocked a cup over, dropped a knife on the floor. She hovered impotently as if faced by a build-up of problems she had no hope of solving. She was too confused even to weep and had to give up and somehow find her way to bed. She must have drifted off to sleep eventually because she was awakened by Charlie's astonished voice.

"My dinner's not ready. You haven't even washed the dishes. Are you ill or something?"

She stared up at him, his cropped grey head, his loose hanging jowls.

"Oh, Charlie."

"What's wrong?" He sat down on the bed groping for her hand.

"I'm so depressed," she said.

He rolled his eyes heaven-wards, relief dispelling his anxiety. "Is that all?"

Tears spurted out and rushed down her face.

"This is ridiculous," Charlie said. "You'll just have to snap out of it. Helen's happy. What have you got to worry about?"

Not getting any reply, he patted her hand and added in a kinder tone, "You've got me. I'll always be here."

31

"I'm sorry, Charlie."

"Here take my hanky." It was none too clean. "Go on," Charlie urged.

Miserably, daintily, she dabbed at her tears.

"I know the very thing," Charlie said. "A cup of tea in bed."

"No, thank you, dear."

"Well, I'll do the dishes for you while you're cooking the dinner. Then we'll just have a nice quiet night watching telly, eh?"

She nodded but was unable to control another overflow of tears.

"Now, come on, Annie, pull yourself together."

She hated being called that. She had never felt like an "Annie". Long ago she had told him this but it was as if the name Ann stuck in his throat or was some sort of embarrassment. He could never bring himself to say it. Instead, he never called her anything. Or he referred to her as the "old woman", or "old wife", or "the wife".

"I'll be all right in a minute."

"I'll tell you what. I'll run down for a couple of fish suppers and that'll save you cooking. How about that, eh?" His voice seemed even louder than usual. It bruised her brain and made it difficult to think.

"All right, dear," she managed.

"And don't say I'm not good to you. Come on them, snap out of it. Hurry up and get the table set. We haven't much time before the news comes on."

She went through to the kitchen table and began fumbling with the dishes again. She could hear Charlie whistling as he went down the stairs.

Chapter Seven

LETHARGY DRAGGED at her heels. Never before in her life had she experienced such a weight of tiredness. She struggled to whip herself alert, sharpen her attention, energize her limbs, but it was as if she was being sucked deeper and deeper, darker and darker into a muddy bog.

"You're going about like a half-shut knife," Charlie complained. "It's making my life a misery the way you're carrying on."

"I'm not doing it on purpose, Charlie."

"It's time you pulled yourself together, snapped out of it, gave yourself a jerk."

"I can't seem to get organized any more."

"You've all the time in the world now, and there's only the two of us, yet you say you can't get things done. Just look at the dust on that sideboard. It's ridiculous."

"Oh, what does it matter?"

"What do you mean, 'What does it matter'?"

"We'll be away at Millport for the next two weeks."

"You're turning into a slut and there's absolutely no excuse for it. Look at Sadie Hennessy next door and just think yourself lucky."

"Oh, sure."

"We'll never get away to Millport at this rate."

"Everything's packed."

"No thanks to you. I did most of it."

"I never asked you. I was doing it."

"You had the case shut and all the new stuff lying through in the kitchen; my new sponge and face cloth, my new vest and pants. . . ."

"All right. All right."

"No, it's not all right. I don't know what's come over you. You're determined to spoil my holiday. I work hard and all I've to look forward to is my holiday at Millport. . . ."

"Let's go then." She almost added, "And get it over with," but contained herself in time.

It wasn't that she had anything against Millport. Each time the boat from the mainland approached the small island, her mind registered how pretty it was, set like an emerald in a sapphire-blue water. Everything about it sparkled with cleanliness despite the hordes of wildly happy children, busy with pails and spades, or ice-cream cones. There were very few cars on the island but strings of horses from the riding stables clopped leisurely along. An abundance of bicycles careered about joyfully ringing bells. Several shops on the front had great tangles of them inside and outside. It was one of the "musts" of Millport, to hire a bike and cycle round the island. Charlie could hardly wait to heave his hefty backside on to the saddle. She had long suspected, however, that it was not so much the exercise he enjoyed or the trip round the island, but the laugh he got at her struggles to keep up with him. Often he nearly fell off his bicycle with hilarity, and the slower or more tired she became, the more riotous his pleasure. It had developed into a test of endurance, as if his manhood was at stake, or as if there was a fortune in prize money waiting for the winner.

Apart from cycling, they didn't do very much, except have a ritual game of crazy golf at which Charlie also loved to win, and a paddle in the water. Charlie rolled up his trouser legs and waded in with a kind of ecstasy as if he was being given absolution from the holy Ganges. For the rest of the time they stretched out on the sand if it was hot, and Charlie protected his head with a knotted handkerchief. If it was a cooler day they sat on one of the benches on the promenade. It tickled Charlie to make remarks about people who passed by or who were cavorting on the sand or in the water. But he seldom spoke *to* anyone. If someone addressed him he answered easily enough but he never took the initiative. He seemed perfectly content to remain exclusively in her company. It was as if they were still sitting alone in front of television.

Nevertheless, the change of scene and the good fresh air lifted her depression a little. Even the change of sink helped. Charlie didn't like hotels or boarding-houses and they always rented the same ancient flat for a couple of weeks.

"We can go in and out as we like with nobody to bother us," he always said.

It meant she had to do her own cooking and cleaning, and in circumstances far more primitive and spartan than she was used to. There was no freezer or fridge, no stainless-steel sink, no pretty china, no fashionable furniture and certainly no electric blankets here. The bare minimum for survival was contained in a piece of paper nailed to the flaky kitchen wall. It listed each Woolworth's mug and piece of tinny cutlery and ended with a warning that any articles broken or missing must be paid for.

Sunshine reached some of the bleak places of her mind and heart and coaxed them back to life. She found herself able to gossip with Charlie about the passers-by and even laugh with him.

Then the rain came. It didn't keep them in during the day, because, as usual, they had come prepared with wellington-boots and plastic macs and hats. They still strolled about and sat on the benches, but it wasn't the same with water continuously trickling down your face and neck. More and more they sheltered in cafés. She lost count of how many teas, coffees, lemonades and ices they consumed. At night they munched sweets and watched television. She had never been so thankful when a holiday came to an end. Yet, a great tidal wave of depression carried her back to the mainland.

"That's good old Millport until next year," Charlie said. "Roll on next year."

That night, as usual, they met the Hennessys in the pub, and Charlie told them how "Good Old Millport" was still the same as ever and what a marvellous time they'd had.

On the Sunday they had been invited over to Helen and Dave's for dinner and Charlie went through his whole story about Millport again, almost word for word. By the time the meal was finished and they were all sitting around the electric fire, he and Helen were at the reminiscing stage, working their way further and further back through the Millports of previous years. Dave seemed fascinated and was eager and ready to laugh at the slightest sign of Charlie's or Helen's laughter.

The Millport nostalgia was abruptly cut off by the ending of the

34

religious programme. Dave went over and turned up the sound. The next programme didn't happen to be anything they fancied so they talked absentmindedly above it, at the same time keeping their eyes glued to the box.

"I'll help you with the dishes, Helen," Ann said.

"No hurry, Mum. Dave can help me with them later."

"Don't listen to her, Mrs Sommerville," Dave said. "Dave's not going to touch the dishes. Dish-washing's a woman's work."

Charlie laughed. "Well said, Dave. Let them get on with it. Be the boss in your own house."

Helen ignored her father. "You've a nerve, Dave, I work in a shop the same as you. I work the same hours as you. It's only fair we should take equal shares of the work at home."

"Equal shares?" Dave turned to Charlie; "I've made every stick of furniture in here. See that wall unit. . . ."

"Oh, stuff your bloody wall unit," Helen said before flouncing from the room.

Ann followed her into the kitchen.

"How's the new job doing, Helen? Is it a busy shop? What are the other assistants like?"

"Male chauvinist pig! He makes the furniture because he *wants* to make furniture, because he *likes* to make furniture. That's him all over. He just does what he bloody likes!"

Helen crashed dishes about in the sink. Ann looked anxious.

"There's always little difficulties at the beginning, Helen, adjustments to be made until you get used to each other's ways."

"Male chauvinist pig!"

"We all have our bad points but as long as you love Dave, I'm sure that. . . ." Burning beacons of hatred seared round at her.

"I love Eric."

"Helen!"

"Why the shocked expression? I told you I loved Eric. I told you I'd always love Eric."

Ann didn't know what to say. She was appalled.

Then Charlie bawled from the other room. "Hurry up, you two. You'll miss the film."

Chapter Eight

"FOR GOD'S sake, go to the Bingo," Charlie said. Maybe that'll liven you up."

At first she didn't reply and Charlie said, "You're either going off your nut or you're even more stupid than I thought you were. Of course, you were always a bit queer. I suppose 'the change' is just making you queerer."

Still she could not bring herself to speak.

"Well, stupid, if you go now you'll catch Sadie before she leaves. But don't make this a habit, do you hear? If you go again go in the afternoon. I've suffered enough without being left here by myself all night while you go gallivanting off to the Bingo. Go on then!"

She could have killed him. Only she hadn't the energy and anyway she knew he meant well. He was trying, in his own way, to help her. Shakily she went for her anorak and had left the house and knocked on Sadie Hennessy's door before she realized she hadn't brought her handbag. She rang her own bell and Charlie's door opened at the same time as Sadie's.

"I forgot my handbag, Charlie."

"I told you, you're going queer."

"There it is on the hall table."

"Did you knock at my door, Mrs Sommerville?" asked Sadie.

Charlie gave a jerk of his head in Ann's direction. "She wants you to take her to the Bingo."

"Oh, sure, sure. You're welcome, Mrs Sommerville."

Ann was quick to sense the extra loudness of her neighbour's words and the effort needed to push out their welcoming brightness. She forced out bright words herself as Sadie collected her coat then they both went to meet Nellie Murtie.

They entered the foyer of what once had been the Rexy Cinema.

"Get your money out, hen," Nellie said kindly to Ann. "This is where you get your books."

Nellie went before her in the queue at the cash desk, blocking it completely with her shapeless mountain of fat. Ann found her purse and held it at the ready. She sensed dedication and ruthless efficiency about the people in the queue, despite Nellie's indulgence, although on entering the huge hall she was still taken aback by the sea of intensity swamping the rows of red plastic tables and benches. A glitter of many red and yellow lights showed up in depressing detail the pale faces, the crushed headscarves and the cotton coats, the overflowing ashtrays, the purple carpet awash with plastic cups, empty cigarette and crisp packets.

She followed Nellie and Sadie through the gilt pillars right down one of the aisles to a table at the front. From everywhere a record was blaring, "Bingo, bingo, I'm in love!" Sadie gave her instructions on how to play then proceeded to initial each of her own cards with the names of her children.

"That's to bring me luck," she explained.

Up on a stage a dapper young man in a black dinner–jacket and black bow–tie took his position behind what looked like a pulpit of studded purple velvet. Alongside him, on a purple stand, was a

36

glass box in which ping–pong balls, each with a number on it, whirled airily around.

"All the fives, fifty–five," he called through a stunningly efficient microphone. "Number six, on its own."

Ann marvelled at the way everyone's pen glided effortlessly up and down columns of figures checking off the numbers rapidly being called out. It was also a mystery at first how any mistake the young man made was immediately detected and pounced on, until she realized that, as well as having a TV screen on his "pulpit", there were screens in every corner of the hall that recorded each ball and its number when it was ejected from the whirl in the glass box.

"You want a loan of my glasses, Jimmy?" someone would shout. Or: "Away and rumble your balls, Jimmy!"

She appreciated the humour that kept sparking up but her ability to smile and even join in laughter did nothing to dispel her depression. She was glad when the interval came and as well as buying new cards one could purchase a drink or a cup of tea. Some people had brought flasks and sandwiches and looked as if they had been there all day.

Nellie drank her tea standing beside the table so that she could "have a stretch". Jerking her head in the direction of the stage she observed, above the strains of "Bingo, bingo, I'm in love . . .", "I think his eyes are in his arse."

"His mind's not on the job," Sadie agreed.

The music stopped and everyone settled down to concentrate on the serious business of the evening again. Ann's pen wandered over the numbers on her card until somebody shouted, "House!" Then while one of the girl attendants in a red jersey and gold dangling earrings ran to collect the card to have it checked, she rose, "You'll have to excuse me. It must be the heat in here. I feel a bit faint. I'll have to go out for a breath of air."

Nellie said, "Do you want one of us to come with you, hen?"

"No, no. I'll just take my time and walk home. Don't worry. Goodbye."

Her eyes clung to the littered carpet all the way back up the aisle. At last she completed her escape. Out in the night street she took the correct turning more by luck than right judgement. She felt distressed beyond understanding. Thankfully she arrived at her own door.

Charlie heard her key. "I'll put the kettle on," he said, passing her in the lobby. "You're just in time for the beginning of 'Blankety–Blank'. By the way, Helen phoned."

"Is she all right?"

"Why shouldn't she be?"

37

"I was worried. Things didn't seem very happy between her and Dave."

"It's none of your business how things are between her and Dave. Come on, get the cups out. Do something for your keep! Did you have a good time at the Bingo?" he asked as he carried the teapot through and she followed with the tray.

"No."

"That's good."

She glanced across and saw that he was no longer listening. The quiz game had started.

"I think I'll go to bed," she said eventually.

"You're always going to bed these days. What's up with you?"

"I'm tired, that's all."

"You don't do anything. How can you be tired?"

"I clean the house and make the meals and. . . ."

"Don't be daft! That's nothing. What would you be like if you had a job?"

"Useless?" she queried bitterly.

He laughed again.

"That's right. Come here, stupid." Grabbing her hand he jerked her down beside him on to the settee. "Watch 'Blankety-Blank' and shut up."

"Charlie, I don't feel well."

"You're working yourself into a tizzy over your kid. It's ridiculous. It's time you pulled yourself together and gave yourself a shake."

"And snapped out of it?"

Despite herself, tears came to her eyes and her voice quavered. "I just want her to be happy."

Charlie sighed and put his arm around her shoulders.

"Of course she'll be happy. Why shouldn't she be happy?"

She didn't answer and his attention strayed back to watching television even though it was now a programme he was not interested in.

Because she's married to the wrong man? she wondered. But if she was so in love with Eric, what went wrong? Why didn't she marry him? Misunderstandings happened, she supposed. And when you were young you were touchy and impulsive and sometimes did the wrong things for what you thought were the right reasons.

She and Joel had misunderstandings. Why hadn't she come right out and told him she loved him and no messing about? That last night she should have told him she loved him and didn't know how she was going to live without him. Was it shyness that had not only kept these words back but made her say instead an almost casual

38

goodbye to him? After he'd gone to sea that time they had exchanged a few letters. How strange to think of them now, with the strips cut out of every page by a wartime censor. Then the letters had stopped. Even now she could hardly bear to recall the agony of bewilderment she had suffered and the longing for him. She wrote letter after letter, trying in them, every way she could think of, to elicit a response. Any kind of response. But she never received a reply to any of her letters.

As she sat next to Charlie in front of the television Joel became more poignantly real to her than him.

Chapter Nine

NEXT DAY she left him a note. It said, "Dear Charlie, your dinner's in the oven. I've gone over to see Helen. I couldn't sleep last night with worrying about her. I'll try not to be late. Love from Ann."

Once at the huge housing estate, she wandered about for what seemed hours before finding the right tower block of flats. The concrete monsters looked all the same to her. She didn't like any of them. The lifts were a particular bugbear. As the doors clanged together, sealing her in a solid steel box she suffered claustrophobia. At the fourteenth floor she was ready to hasten out immediately the doors opened. The landing, however, was as claustrophobic as the lift, boxed in by four doors, each with a glass "eye" glinting coldly at her. There seemed something indicative of the times about the new tenement blocks. There never had been any need for spy-holes in the old flats.

For a few minutes she hesitated at Helen's door before ringing the bell. She hadn't a clue about what she was going to do or say once inside the house. No idea how she could help or comfort Helen.

The bell gave a sudden rasping sound. Then there was a long silence. She tried to compose her features into a pleasing expression as if the spy-hole were taking her picture.

At last the door opened and Helen announced in a voice she seemed to have been rehearsing, "Oh, hello, Mum. What a surprise. Come in. Come on through," Helen said, still in the stagey voice, and at the same time opening the living-room door.

"It's my mum, everybody. Just popped in for an unexpected visit."

"Everybody" was a room packed with young people. They were crushed together on the settee, on the chairs, on the floor. Curtains shut out the summer evening's light and only the orange wax bubbles and a red spotlight feebly elbowed at the shadows. It was smoky too and stank of beer and whisky. What had obviously been a "swinging" party had suddenly died. Eventually the strain of embarrassment forced out polite greetings. Brightly, Ann interrupted them.

"Can't stay I'm afraid. Charlie's waiting downstairs in the car. Just dashed up with a message for Helen. Bye, now!"

"Oh," Helen visibly relaxed with relief and shut the room door again. "Dad's waiting, is he? That's all right, then. Were the pair of you out for a run?"

"Yes, it was such a lovely night. Sorry to barge into your party, dear. I just thought I'd pop up with these biscuits I baked. Well, I didn't exactly bake them today. I took them out the freezer but I knew they were your favourites and I just thought — when I was passing. . . ."

"Thanks, Mum."

Dave came out with a pint of beer in his hand and stood with an arm around Helen's shoulder at the front door.

"Sure you haven't time for a cup of tea, Mrs Sommerville?"

"No, I must dash. Thanks all the same, Dave. Bye!"

The lift doors gaped open like steel jaws. She pressed the button and sank down to the ground floor. Somehow she got back home to Canal Lane.

"You were quick," Charlie said. "Did they give you your walking ticket?"

"Is there any tea left?" She lowered herself on to the settee beside him.

A cocky, fast-talking comedian was on television and Charlie couldn't quite unglue his atention or his laugh.

"Just a minute. He's good, this chap." He coughed out a loud guffaw, with a cloud of pipe smoke then absently added, "I'll make you one at the commercials."

As soon as the commercial break came on he got up.

"Do you want a cream puff or a jam doughnut?"

"Nothing to eat, thanks."

"Look, I've told you before there's no use you taking it out on me."

"I just don't want anything to eat, Charlie."

"Don't give me that. You always have a cake at night."

A flame began licking up inside her head. "Yes, every single night."

"What's that supposed to mean?"

"It means I'm bloody sick of eating bloody stupid cakes every night."

"Oh, charming, just charming. You go poking your nose in where it's not wanted and just because you get it put in a sling you come home and take your spite out on me. And just watch your language. I'll have none of your bad language in here."

She hated him. Just over a lousy cake, she felt burned up with hatred. Not daring to argue and allow her emotions full rein she took a deep breath and in a smooth voice said, "All right, Charlie. I'll have a jam doughnut."

Sucking with satisfaction at his pipe he plodded through to the kitchen to fetch a tray. She tried not to think about his checked carpet slippers and bulging belly. Or his shirt with its rolled-up sleeves and loosened top button and tie. Or the smell of hot sweat from him. Charlie didn't believe in deodorants. At least, not for men. He thought it was sissy.

"Here you are," said Charlie when he returned, thrusting a steaming mug of tea and a jam doughnut under her nose. He added, "And don't say I'm not good to you."

The programme finished. The picture shrivelled into a spot and disappeared. Charlie switched off at the set then pulled out the plug from the wall.

"Another lousy night," he said. "I don't know where they dig up all the rubbish they put on."

He knocked out his pipe in the nearest ashtray. "Half of these TV blokes should be put up against a wall and shot. I could do better myself. Well? Are you going to sit there all night? Come on, you can tell me what happened at Helen's while we're getting ready for bed."

Bedtime was talking time. Sometimes Charlie talked while they were making love. He carried on a perfectly ordinary, mundane conversation except that it was slightly more jerky and breathless.

Charlie chortled at the idea of her gate-crashing a young people's party.

"I'd love to have seen your face. And I bet their faces were worth seeing as well. I can just hear the groans of them. An old woman putting a damper on their high jinks. That was a turn-up for the book!"

"You're maybe an old man, Charlie," she said, "but I'm not an old woman."

Charlie chuckled. "You're not just any old woman. You're *my* old woman. Now stop worrying and go to sleep."

She did sleep eventually and the next thing she knew, Charlie was shaking her and saying, "Are you going to lie there all day? By God, some folk are lucky. I wish I could have a lie back. Here's a cup of tea. And don't say I'm not good to you."

Hoisting herself up by her elbows she stared dazedly at the alarm clock.

"Yes," said Charlie. "You're going to make me late for my work.

41

Here, take the tea and don't spill it all over the bed." He gave her a quick kiss. "OK?"

"OK," she said.

"The laugh is," he told her later that day after he'd finished work, "you were the one who wanted to get up and make my breakfast. You can't even make your own breakfast. Never mind mine."

"I know," she tried to laugh along with him. "I'm useless."

"And as for finding a job — I could have told you that no one would have you. You're far too old, Annie."

She was holding the iron stew pot and dishing more steak and onions on to his plate. Suddenly, with all her strength, she crashed the pot down on the table. She imagined it was a sledge-hammer on Charlie's skull. A plate broke with a high cracking sound like a scream. Stew pelted over the table and splattered Charlie's blue-striped shirt with brown. He reared up like a bear, arms hanging wide, bewildered eyes down on his chest.

"Look what you've done to my good shirt! And it's roasting hot as well."

"Take it off."

"I'm burned right through."

She unbuttoned his shirt as if he were a child, then rubbed his chest with her apron. "It's hardly touched you."

"Look at the table. Look at all the mess."

"I'll clean it up."

"And what did you do it for?"

"I don't know."

"You're mad!"

"Go over to the settee and watch television, Charlie."

"I haven't had any pudding yet."

"You can eat your pudding over there. I'll bring it through."

"Stark raving mad!"

In the kitchen she dished the rice pudding and put it on a tray with a spoon and a large jug of milk. Charlie liked a lot of milk with his rice pudding.

Later she took another tray through and a cloth and a basin of water.

"What are you doing now?" Charlie asked.

"Clearing up the mess."

"You ought to be ashamed."

"Yes, Charlie."

"I can't even get peace to watch 'Coronation Street' any more."

"I won't be five minutes."

"That's what you always say."

"I'll get you another shirt."

"You've never content. You can't sit still. . . ."

42

In a way she was glad that this was their pub night. Maybe a few drinks would pull her together. No sherry. A few good *strong* drinks.

Charlie was still nagging at her when they eventually got to the pub.

"You know what she did tonight?"

He could hardly wait to tell the Hennessys who were already seated at their favourite corner table.

Sadie looked sympathetic.

"Your nerves just got the better of you, Mrs Sommerville."

"What's *she* got nerves for?" Charlie wanted to know.

"Never mind, hen." Willy Hennessy rubbed his hands. "A wee drink'll soon cure your nerves. The usual, eh?"

"Yes," Charlie answered. "A pint of heavy for me and a sherry for her."

"No, a large gin and bitter lemon for me."

"But you always take sherry," Charlie protested.

"I don't like sherry."

"Don't be daft. You love sherry."

Ignoring Charlie she kept staring at Willy Hennessy with a smile stitched to her face.

"A large gin and bitter lemon, please," she repeated, her eyes daring him to get her anything else.

"OK! OK!" Willy flung up his hands in mock surrender. "A gin and bitter lemon it is!"

It tasted good. It helped her to relax, blunting the cutting edge of her thoughts and taking away some of the pain. She was able to nurse herself in secret, cocoon herself in isolation from the people around her, not be irritated by their conversation although still hearing it.

They talked about the weather, about the holidays, about the Bingo, about their favourite programmes on "telly", and about football.

Willy Hennessy and some of his other mates always went to matches. Charlie was perfectly content to watch them on television.

Now they had got on to the subject of the war.

"Remember the letters you used to send?" Sadie asked her husband.

"I used to try all sorts of tricks to let her know where I was and what was going on," Willy explained.

"But the censor still cut bits out. You tried to tell me about D-day, didn't you, Willy?"

"I knew there was something building up."

"You weren't allowed to write at all eventually, were you, Willy?"

43

"She was furious, you know. She thought I was to blame."

"For D-day?" Charlie said.

Willy laughed, "No, for not writing." His eyes became vague with remembering.

"Gold Beach, Juno Beach, Sword Beach. That's what they were called then. That's where the British and the Canadians landed and that's where a lot of them died."

"You were lucky to get back home, weren't you, Willy?"

In Joel's last letters there had been references to some sort of build-up. Many ships, including his own, were massing at –. The censor had cut out where.

It had never occurred to her before that Joel could be dead. She could not recall the idea ever entering her mind. Even now, it did not seem possible. It was too cruel. Visions of the circumstances in which he could have died flicked across her line of vision like a horror movie. She could not bear the idea of his being hurt or killed.

Why had she never thought of the possibility at the time? Stumbling back to wartime and herself as an immature teenager she realized that in the selfishness of youth she had only thought of herself. Her longing for him to be with her, her need to hear his voice, to feel the touch of his hand, to see the love and tenderness in his eyes. All these things had obsessed her. She had dreamed of their lives being forever entwined. Youth had no thoughts of death. At least, not in this city at that particular time. No doubt the newspapers and news bulletins had also been censored. She had been thoughtless and selfish — yes, *but at the time* surely no one knew about Gold Beach, Juno Beach, Sword Beach and the ships which carried the men to these beaches, and the sailors who manned the ships.

Joel had been a naval commando. She remembered feeling very proud of this. Without knowing exactly what the term meant she had been sure it must refer to Joel being one of the fittest and toughest and most élite members of the Canadian Navy.

The lean body took shape before her eyes. She saw the strong tanned neck. The smiling eyes. He was so young.

If only they'd made love that last night. If only she'd told him how she'd felt. Much later she had confessed in a letter.

For a minute her thoughts froze in mid-air. Then they painfully splintered. Before that last desperate letter confessing her love for him, there had been other letters. In one she had tried to incite a response from him by making him jealous. Such a stupid letter it had been. It had taken the form of an ultimatum. She had pretended that there had been another man who was in love with her and had asked her to marry him. "If I don't get a prompt reply to this letter," she'd written — or words to that effect, "I'll accept his offer and become engaged to him." She could not remember exactly what she'd said but thinking back now it seemed such a stupid, cruel letter.

What if Joel had received it just before plunging into the holocaust of the D-day landings?

Her eyes closed, bringing a curtain down in her mind.

Chapter Ten

SHE WAS tempted to sleep the rest of her life away. Lying in bed with curtains muffling sound and holding back the moving light, she floated in thoughtless limbo.

Sometimes she became aware that Charlie was due home and the urgency to have his lunch ready gave her enough impetus to drag herself up. But after he left the house again she returned to her blanket burrow. She could only force herself back to the kitchen at the last minute to prepare his evening meal.

She ate little. The sound of the television was like chalk squeaking continuously across the blackboard of her nerves. She could hardly wait to escape from it.

"This is ridiculous," Charlie shouted in exasperation. "You can't go to bed! It's not seven o'clock yet."

"I'm tired."

"How can you be tired?"

"I don't know."

"You don't do anything. You *can't* be tired."

She made for the bedroom, mind obsessed with sleep. In the dusk of the curtained room she was content for lethargy to drag her into mindless paralysis. But within minutes Charlie came staggering into the room carrying the television.

"I'll plug it in here and you can watch it in bed," he panted. "And don't say I'm not good to you."

She took a sleeping tablet while Charlie was organizing a chair for himself close to the bed. Soon she had the vague idea she was in a fairground. Raucous music whirled about along with a confusion of voices until eventually the tablet allowed her to escape into unconsciousness.

Life might have gone on like this. Only, the freezer ran out of food for Charlie's dinner. Guilt roused her to leave the house and automatically make her way to the butcher's. Afterwards she wandered in to the delicatessen and purchased some quiche. Wondering what it would taste like stirred her a little. She even found enough energy to visit the library. It was while she was wandering around the shelves that she noticed the leaflets and brochures. Picking one up she began to idly flick through it. It was advertising extra-mural activities run by the university and one class caught her eye and alerted her senses. It was a class on Literary Appreciation and the tutor was Simon Edgington. She had forgotten all about it. Now here it was beginning this very afternoon.

In a rush of nervous energy she hurried back to the house. She set the table ready for the evening meal then changed into a clean blouse. The venue was within walking distance and she set out, hot and breathless, completely at the mercy of an emotional see-saw. She didn't know whether she felt happy or terrified.

She discovered that the class met in a room of a converted terrace house — one of many houses in the district now owned by the university. Slipping into a back seat she fixed her eyes on the patch of floor at her feet. The room was lively with conversation and a few tentative glances around revealed that there were more women than men and, with the exception of a few women in their thirties and a couple of younger students, most of the others were over forty.

"Is this your first time?" the woman next to her asked.

"Yes. At least to this class it is."

"I'm Jessie Tait."

"Ann Sommerville."

They shook hands.

"Have you been to one of this tutor's classes before, Mrs Tait?"

"Jessie."

"Jessie."

"Oh, yes." Jessie giggled. "He's absolutely marvellous. A real sexy beast. He wouldn't have to ask me twice!"

Jessie gave her a triple nudge. "Here he is."

Ann felt a sense of shock at seeing him again at such close quarters. It wasn't just his appearance. It was as if the concentrated essence of him was piercing her like a laser beam even though he never glanced at her as he strolled down the passage between the desks.

Leaning his bottom against the table facing the class he looked gravely at everyone in turn. As if receiving a message from his eyes, the class fell silent.

"Good afternoon," he said, then after a moment added, "I see we have two new ladies." He fixed his attention on a woman in a faded black coat in the front row.

"Welcome to the class." Somehow he managed to make the words sound like, "You fascinating creature," and at the same time look as if he was in earnest. "Your name is?"

46

"Mrs Abby Thomson."

"We're all on first-name terms here. Do you mind?"

The woman had a tremble which made her head nod. But she said, "No."

"I'm glad you decided to join us, Abby. And the lady at the back?"

Grey eyes gazed questioningly over the heads of the others.

"Ann Sommerville."

"I believe we've met before, Ann. It's good to see you again. I hope you'll enjoy the course."

She flushed with pleasure and felt a sudden wild palpitation of the heart. But his attention had left her and he was telling the class that the author they would be studying this session would be D.H. Lawrence. He gave a list of paperback books which they all wrote down. She looked forward to buying them and reading them. During the first hour, before the coffee break, she couldn't take her eyes off Simon Edgington. But, unlike the woman next to her, her intense interest had nothing to do with the tutor as a man — at least not in a sexual way. It had to do with learning, the actual soaking up of information and opinions and quotations she had never heard before.

The tutor's attention seemed to alternate between an intense projected interest and a turning inwards that left a vague impression that he wasn't there in the same room as the students at all. Ann sensed this subtle withdrawal as he read from D.H Lawrence,

"'It is the way our sympathy flows and recoils that really determines our lives. And here lies the vast importance of the novel, properly handled. It can inform and lead into new places the flow of our sympathetic consciousness, and it can lead our sympathy away in recoil from things gone dead . . . it can reveal the most secret places of life.'"

But afterwards he seemed to come back to them. He invited comments and the class, surprised and encouraged by his apparent interest in what they said, became more and more voluble. So carried away in fact did they become that the coffee break was forgotten. The janitor, who liked to get the dishes washed and knock off early, had to batter on the room door and shout indignantly, "Coffee!"

The formal discussion ended in a burst of surprised laughter. Then everyone, chattering among one another, moved towards the corridor. They had been transformed into enthusiastic schoolchildren. Mothers and grandmothers giggled. "Wasn't what I said awful?"

But they were obviously delighted with their utterances. They assured each other they could just die with embarrassment. But obviously they had never been more happily alive for years.

Ann thought it both pathetic and fascinating. To become so excited about getting the chance to talk and to be listened must mean that normally they must lead very dull, repressed lives. But Simon Edgington not only drew them out but manipulated them. No matter how inarticulate someone sounded. No matter what inane words groped out, Simon listened with as much intentness as if the person had been a professor of literature. Then he would gravely announce, "Jessie has made a good point. Her thesis is. . . ."

His paraphrasing and elucidation of whatever Jessie or Peg or Frank or Bob or Bella had or had not been trying to say was a work of art in in itself.

But when a group of big-bosomed matrons hemmed him in against the stairs and fought for talking time over the coffee cups, he remained, to all appearances, untouched by their emotion, an oasis of calm.

Ann collected her cup from the long wooden table that the janitor had set up in the corridor. Standing by herself she sipped the hot coffee and looked around. A couple of times she caught the tutor's eye. Just for a second or two over the heads of the others, he favoured her with a quizzical stare.

Back in the room after the coffee was finished, he hitched himself on to the desk and gazed around the class until everyone was quietly settled. Then he continued his lecture which again was followed by a general discussion. The audacity to take part in this verbal adventure was completely beyond Ann. Yet her enjoyment and participation was none the less intense. Afterwards hurrying home she was still joyfully contributing in her thoughts.

A surge of energy helped her not only to cook Charlie's dinner but to attack an enormous pile of ironing while she was waiting for him to arrive. It was obvious, when he did come into the kitchen to hang his jacket behind the door, that he was pleased to see her energetically working. When they kissed, she hung affectionately for a few seconds round his neck.

"Oh, Charlie, I had such a lovely time this afternoon. It was so *interesting!*"

"At the Bingo, were you?"

"No, an extra-mural class."

"A what?" The happy indulgence faded from his eyes.

"On Literary Appreciation."

"What are you wasting your time on that rubbish for?"

"We were studying D.H. Lawrence. That's not rubbish. He was the one who wrote. . . ."

"I know what he wrote. I'm not daft. He wrote dirty books."

"Charlie!"

"It's the truth. These egg-heads up at the Uni can maybe fool you with all their high-falutin' talk. But a dirty book's a dirty book."

"Well, I haven't read the books yet but today the tutor was telling us quite a bit about D.H. Lawrence as a man. All about his life and how it affected his writing and. . . ."

"He ran away with another man's wife. And she was a German as well. I don't need to waste my time going up to the Uni and listening to some poof tell me anything about D.H. Lawrence."

"It was so *interesting*, Charlie. I enjoyed it. I felt I was learning something."

Charlie shook his head. "You didn't know about D.H. Lawrence? How stupid can you get? I've known about that fruit and nut case for years. Why didn't you ask me? It could have saved you all that bother."

"You don't understand. It wasn't any bother. There was this discussion, Charlie. You ought to have heard it. I just wish you'd been there. . . ."

"Where's my dinner?"

"I'm just going to dish it. You would have seen and heard how. . . ."

"What is it?"

"Steak."

"I hope there's potatoes. I like potato. And none of that dried stuff that you mash up. I like a real potato. I'll carry mine through.

"All right." She arranged steak, brussel sprouts and potatoes on a plate then followed him into the front room carrying her own dinner.

"They were mostly all about our age."

"Who?"

"The people at the class."

"Well, they were old enough to have more sense."

"What has sense got to do with it?"

"Sitting there listening to some poof natter on about a nutter that's been dead and buried for donkey's years."

"His work's still alive."

"These Uni guys have to do something to kid folk they're earning their money. And all they can do is jaw." He went over and switched on the television.

"I learned something."

"So you know something about D.H. Lawrence. So what?"

It was as if he had pulled a plug and allowed all her energy to fritter away. In a matter of seconds she had barely enough strength to keep on breathing. A dead weight pressed down on her and she did not care enough to try to lift it. Time wafted heedlessly past until eventually, from a distance, she heard Charlie say, "Hurry up, the commercials are on. Time to do the dishes. That programme gets worse every week. Talk about money for old rope. The guy that wrote that programme should be put up against a wall and shot."

"Why do you watch it?"

"There's nothing good on the other side."

"Why don't you switch it off?"

"Well, anything's better than looking at a blank screen."

"Charlie. . . ."

"What?"

"Oh, never mind." She didn't have enough energy to argue.

Chapter Eleven

"READING again?" Charlie said.

"Your lunch is ready. I've just to pour the tea."

"You'll ruin your eyes reading so much."

"I had my glasses on."

"You'll be needing new glasses next."

"There's your rolls."

"Anybody would think I was made of money. How much did this cost?"

He picked up her book. "Over a pound for a paperback?" he roared incredulously.

"Paperbacks are all about that price nowadays. I don't like all of this, Charlie. *The Trespasser* it's called. But some of it's really good. It'll be interesting to hear what the tutor says this afternoon but it seems to me that Lawrence is terrific at describing nature. I think he. . . ."

Finding herself talking to the opened pages of the *Daily News,* her voice frittered away. But after a minute or two she spoke again, this time with much bitterness.

"You're a rude, ignorant man, Charlie."

He cracked the paper down and she saw that he was not only outraged but hurt. Hopelessness swamped the bitterness in her voice.

"Never listening to me when I talk to you. Always putting your paper up like that . . . ."

"You talk all the time. What do you want me to do? Hang on your every word? At that rate I'd never get a look at my paper. You know your trouble? You haven't enough to worry you. That's your trouble. If you had a houseful of kids to worry about like Sadie

Hennessy next door you wouldn't have time to attack me for no reason at all. It's just too bad if a man can't get a bit of peace in his own home after working hard since the crack of dawn. Working hard for money that you fritter away in whatever way takes your fancy."

He clattered back his chair and rose with such violence that the tea leapt and splashed from their cups.

"You haven't eaten all your rolls."

"You're enough to put anybody off their food."

"Where are you going?"

"To my work."

"Charlie, don't be silly. Come back and finish your lunch."

"That's all I'm good for it seems. A money machine. I'm clever enough when it comes to paying the rent."

She had never seen him so upset.

"I didn't mean to hurt you."

"I'm not bothered. You don't bother me."

There was something pathetic about Charlie when he was angry. Although he was a heavily built man there seemed to be a child behind his eyes struggling to get out.

"Charlie." She went over and put her arms comfortingly around him. "You're a kind man and a good husband."

"I've always done my best for you."

"I know, dear." She smoothed a hand over his grey stubble of hair. It prickled like a wire brush and sprang immediately back up after her touch. She clung round his neck and he cuddled her close.

"Anything I've ever done has just been for you and Helen. Now we've only got each other."

She was counting the seconds until he let her go. Yet at the same time she regretted her need to be free of him. It was true she didn't want to hurt Charlie.

He returned to the table and sat down. He bit into his remaining roll but didn't lift his paper. Instead he mumbled, "What was the earth-shaking thing you were saying, then?"

Sitting opposite him she lowered her eyes in embarrassment. "Oh, it was nothing really."

"All this fuss about nothing. Come on, spit it out."

"Well, it was just that I admired the way Lawrence described nature. There's a bit here, for instance — 'seen through a train window'."

She picked up the book and began to read aloud: "'Siegmund almost gloated as he smelled the ripe corn, and opened his eyes to its powerful radiation. For a moment he forgot everything amid the forging of red fields of gold in the smithy of the sunset. Like sparks, poppies blew along the railway banks, a crimson train.'"

51

She glanced up and Charlie yawned, making her voice quicken with embarrassment to the end of the passage.

"'Siegmund waited, through the meadows for the next wheat-field. It came like the lifting of yellow-hot metal out of the gloom of darkened grasslands.'"

Shutting the book she pushed it aside. "I thought that was good."

"It's all right," Charlie said. "Can I read my paper now?"

She tried to laugh. "Sure."

For a few days after the last class she had been in two minds whether or not to return. Charlie obviously didn't like her going. But she had become interested in the books. It was also becoming more and more obvious that she and Charlie had different outlooks on life. She wanted to get out and *do* things. She wanted to meet new people, see new places, learn new things. She felt bored and restricted by routine. Charlie seemed to thrive on it.

In the end she decided she had to keep going to the class whether Charlie liked it or not. It became a matter of urgency. A sort of lifeline. She felt at home in the converted room now with its rows of folding seats and blackboard on the wall and table and chair in front of it for the tutor. She knew the other students and they knew her. They were part of a group. They "belonged" together like members of a family who shared the same blood. Only they were freer. It felt good.

"Hello, Jessie."

"Hello, Ann. What did you think of *The Trespasser?*"

She didn't feel in the slightest embarrassed explaining her thoughts and opinions to Jessie. In fact she became so carried away in an exchange between not only Jessie but two women sitting in front who joined in, that she didn't notice Simon Edgington enter the room. Eventually Jessie nudged her into silence.

It gave her quite a thrill when Simon, during the course of his lecture confirmed her view of Lawrence's ability to describe nature.

"It is what Harry T. More calls Lawrence's 'Kinetic Touch'."

On the blackboard he neatly printed the word "Kinetic". Then returning the chalk to the ledge he dusted his fingers clean.

She could imagine that he was a fastidious man. There was a preciseness, an exactness in everything he said and did. He never hurried. She could almost see his mind selecting with scrupulous care each word that would convey exactly what he was thinking. Or exactly as much of what he was thinking as he wished to convey.

He dressed in casual yet expensive-looking clothes. Even when he wore blue jeans they looked tailored to fit him. His shirts, mostly open-necked during the hot weather, were cut to taper from broad shoulders to flat waist. They fitted like another skin — without one wrinkle. They accentuated the hard leanness of him and the whipcord muscles of his arm.

She began to find pleasure in looking at him as well as listening to him. Discovering he had written a book on Joyce Cary she devoured it with interest. Then she found a couple of slim volumes of poetry by him in the library.

"Charlie, you'll never guess!" She burst out when Charlie arrived home after her visit to the library.

"What?"

"I found a couple of books of poems by Simon today."

"Who's Simon?"

"You know!" she chided impatiently.

"No, I don't know."

"Simon Edgington, my tutor."

"Oh, him."

"There's no need to use that tone of voice. He's a very talented man."

"Oh, they're a great bunch up at the Uni. What's so smart about writing a poem? They're not so smart, these guys."

She sighed. "I thought you'd be interested that I'd met a real poet. I mean, normally writers are just names on the covers of books, like creatures from another world. Fancy actually meeting one in the flesh. Don't you think that's exciting?"

"I was writing poems when I was at school. But I grew up."

She sighed again. "I'll bring the dinner through."

"There's no use you sighing like that. It's the truth. Nearly everybody has a go at writing poems when they're young and daft. When they've fallen for some girl maybe. Or more likely when they have split up. You think it's the end of the world then. And you scribble away at daft poems. But if you've any sense you grow out of it."

He went over and switched on the television.

Raising her voice to be heard above it she said, "Simon doesn't strike me as being immature."

"Since when have teachers been called by their first names?"

"Oh, everybody's on first-name terms. It seems to be the accepted thing now. At least at extra-mural classes."

"A lot of nonsense. That's what's wrong with the world today. What's this?"

"What?"

"In among my stew."

"Mushrooms."

"You've spoiled my dinner!"

"I just thought it would be a change from carrots and onion."

"What's wrong with carrots and onion?"

"Nothing, but. . . ."

"Well, then.'

"Oh, give it to me. I'll take it back and dish you another plateful without mushrooms."

"Yes, just you do that."

In the kitchen she could have screamed with frustration. Returning to the front room she put the plate in front of him then sat watching his hands grope for his fork and knife. It was like staring at a stranger. His cropped head, his heavy jowls were features on an alien planet.

A world or strangeness separated them. She folded into herself. And she was reminded of part of the mystical foreword to *Sons and Lovers* that Simon had read to the class.

His voice made an echoing chamber of her mind.

"'Human emotions don't come with a life-long guarantee. . . . And if the man deny, or be too weak, then shall the woman find another man, of greater strength. And if, because of the Word, which is the Law, she does not find another man, nor he another woman, then shall they both be destroyed.'"

Chapter Twelve

SHE HAD never spoken to Simon Edgington. Occasionally an enthusiastic urge to contribute to the class discussion almost bubbled over. But mostly she was content to let off steam chattering to Jessie or to the women in the row in front before the lecture started, or during the coffee break.

Then one day, when she was collecting her coffee from the table she was startled to find him by her side.

"I think you have been avoiding me, Ann."

She looked up at him in surprise. "I've nothing to say to you."

"Ah! That explains it then."

His eyes, sharp with amusement, held hers, plugging her into pleasurable yet dangerous electric currents. She looked away and was thankful for some other students who moved in to vie for his attention. Disturbed, she could no longer concentrate on Jessie's chatter. She fixed her eyes and smile on the wobbly flesh of the other woman's face. But she was detached from her. She became acutely self-concious. As she sipped the hot coffee she worried in case it was turning her nose red.

The shabbiness of the green anorak pained her like a sackcloth and ashes. The polo-neck of her brown sweater restricted her like an iron collar. Easing it surreptitiously from her throat she laughed at something Jessie said. Not because she was aware of any witticism, only that Jessie was laughing.

Later, after the class was over and the people were making for the door, she knew instinctively that Simon wanted to go outside with her. Usually he packed his papers and books neatly into his briefcase while engaged in polite conversation with the students who always surrounded him, then he allowed himself to be accompanied from the room by one or two of his most persistent admirers until eventually he escaped into his car.

This time he did not seem to be making even a pretence of listening to these voluble ladies. His eyes were on her, sending telepathic messages into her head. Panic all but made her run from the room. As it was, she left in undignified haste, bumping into someone on the way and having to give an embarrassed apology.

Outside, she did run and didn't stop until she had turned corners and reached one-way streets along which his car couldn't follow. Once safely home she felt foolish as well as excited. Amused at herself too. She laughed out loud as she made a cup of coffee. Every time she thought of herself racing through the streets she laughed.

She ached to tell Charlie about this crazy exciting incident. Visualizing herself and Charlie enjoying a good laugh together, she hurried to greet him in the lobby.

"Hello, dear. I did the daftest thing just now. . . ."

"Spare me the sordid details till I go to the lav." The frosted-glass door shut in her face.

Defeated, she trailed back to the kitchen. It struck her that, despite her bouts of depression, she must be an incurable optimist. No matter how often she was disappointed, she always hoped for the best, expected they'd be able to share, took it for granted they must have something in common.

"What a lousy day," Charlie said coming into the kitchen and taking off his jacket. "Cold and miserable and now it's started to rain."

"Well, I suppose we can't expect summer all year round."

She carried the plates through on a tray. Charlie followed her.

"Summer? What summer? We never had a summer this year."

"Of course we had a summer. Sit down and eat your chops. I've made a nice gravy with them."

"You never can do anything right, can you?"

"But you told me you liked gravy. The last time you had chops you said. . . ."

"You've always to go to extremes. When I said I liked gravy on my chops I meant just a spot of gravy. I didn't want them drowned in it."

"All right. I'll take some of it off."

"You'll just make a mess of the plate."

"I'll put your chops on a clean plate."

"A clean plate'll be cold."

Suddenly a madness of hysteria leapt to her mouth. Her hands flew up to contain it but high-pitched, jerky screams escaped. They pulled Charlie up from his seat, grey-faced with shock.

"What the hell . . .?"

Just as suddenly the hysteria stopped. She drew a deep breath and said, "You'll be missing the news, Charlie."

"So I will," he cried, taking big urgent strides towards the television set. "You and your carry on!"

Afterwards he switched over to the other channel for "Coronation Street."

She felt physically shattered by her sudden attack of hysteria. Trembling, insecure, afraid of herself she fought to cling to what she had already read of her book as she sat staring at the television screen. She recalled the intensity of Lawrence's writing, the poetic quality, the sensuousness. He was sometimes too intense for her liking. Sometimes reading his work was, she felt, like being drawn into a dark jungle. It wasn't a true picture of life. Life had light as well as darkness, laughter and nonsense as well as gloom and seriousness. Nobody in real life could survive such intense relationships as Lawrence depicted. And wasn't the basic criterion to judge a work of art its relation to real life?

She imagined herself posing this question to Simon Edgington. She began to carry on a discussion with him in her mind.

Surely good writing should give a true picture of human beings. Many of Lawrence's characters did strike a note of absolute truth of course. It seemed to her that these were the characters which stemmed from a background of conflict in Lawrence's own life.

In her mind's eye she formed a cool elegant picture of herself, thoughtfully developing her point. Simon was not only intensely interested but most impressed by what she was saying.

"Consider these facts, Simon. Lawrence's father was a collier, a passive, unambitious man, more at home with sensual experience and basic human relationships with his workmates. Lawrence's mother was a school-teacher, ambitious, genteel, looking outward to wider horizons. She had her own set of cultural and social values which were different from that of the mining community to which her husband belonged. Don't you agree that these conflicting values formed the background to Lawrence's early life and that this pattern of conflict in which the woman is the dominating influence is reflected in much of Lawrence's work?"

"That's an excellent point, Ann. Can you give the class specific

56

illustrations from his work?"

"Certainly. For instance. . . ."

"Time for supper." Charlie's gruff voice startled her. "Come on, I'll put the kettle on while you get the cakes. I fancy a cream sponge. How about you?"

"I don't want one, Charlie. I don't want to get fat."

"Who cares? Enjoy yourself! I'm not going to divorce you if you put on a few pounds."

"*I* care. I don't want to get fat."

"Don't be daft. What difference will a sponge make? Get them out. We'll miss the start of *The Gambling Man*."

She tried to understand why Charlie needed her to do everything he was doing. Why couldn't he be content to have his tea and cakes and leave her to have what she wanted? It occurred to her that all she did want was a cup of Horlicks. Sometimes, unable to sleep during the night, she would rise and tiptoe through to the kitchen to make herself a cup. Often it soothed and relaxed her and she was able to drift off to sleep despite the noise of Charlie's snoring.

"I don't want tea either," she said.

"What do you mean, you don't want tea?"

"I'm going to make myself a cup of Horlicks."

Charlie sighed. "What's wrong with you now?"

"Nothing's wrong with me. I just want a cup of Horlicks and nothing to eat with it." Whipping the Horlicks into a mug, she felt tense with guilt and distress.

Charlie said, "I don't know what I've done to deserve this treatment. All our married life I've tried to be a good husband."

"For pity's sake, Charlie! Who said you were a bad husband?"

"You just don't want anything to do with me any more."

"All I said was I didn't want any tea and cakes."

"No, it's not all you said. You said a lot more the other day."

"Have I to wear sackcloth and ashes for the rest of my life because I called you a rude, ignorant man? How many times am I supposed to apologize?"

"I know some women go queer at the 'change' but you've always been a bit queer. You'd better be careful. You'll be ending up as a permanent patient in the nearest loony bin."

"Will you stop saying that, Charlie? There's nothing wrong with me."

"You're perfect I suppose."

"I didn't mean that."

"You don't know what you mean, any more than you know what you want. You've always been the same."

"I meant I'm not queer."

"Even your own mother won't have anything to do with you."

Grief pushed tears up to her eyes. She shaded them with one hand while her chest went into spasms of heaving.

Charlie immediately took her into his arms and laughed affectionately, "Don't be a silly ass. You know you've always got me. Come on through and sit down. I'll see to your supper."

Afterwards he brought the tray and said, "You'll soon feel better after a nice cup of tea and a cream sponge."

Chapter Thirteen

SHE WOULDN'T mind what she had to suffer from Charlie if only she could be certain that Helen hadn't made a mistake in her marriage. If only she could be certain that Helen didn't still love Eric. She couldn't cope with guilt and she must have been guilty in part at least for Helen's break with Eric and subsequent marriage to Dave. Helen certainly seemed to think so.

Every time she thought of Eric, she remembered Joel. What unhappiness, what pain her stupid letter might have caused. It could indirectly have resulted in his death. She kept thinking of how he could have received it just before his ship went into action. She imagined him emotionally upset by what she'd written and being more careless or reckless in the face of danger than he otherwise might have been.

Guilt gnawed at the foundations of her being, leaving a dangerous insecurity. She did not believe herself capable of any relationships. Even acquaintances like Simon Edgington made her feel anxious and uncertain. The Literary Appreciation class which she had been enjoying so much now contained an element of tension and worry that she did not understand. Her instinct was to run away from it. She decided she could not go back, but she knew it was foolish not to. There was no reason to stop going. Yet for no reason she was afraid to go. When the time came, however, she could not bear the alternative of staying alone and purposeless in the empty house.

She donned her anorak but, catching a glimpse of herself in the wardrobe mirror, hesitated then took it off again. Funny, she'd never noticed before what a shabby old thing it was. It should have been thrown out years ago. Rummaging in the wardrobe through clothes that she never bothered to wear, she found a black trouser suit. With a white sweater it looked very smart. Its tailored lines hugged her waist accentuating its slimness. A little eye make-up and a careful application of lipstick finished the picture. On the way to the class, she tried not to think of Simon Edgington. She didn't want to speak to him. No doubt, seeing she was shy, he was just trying to be kind and helpful by making an attempt to single her out for occasional attention. He was a good teacher and made an effort to involve all the class and encourage them to contribute as much as possible.

On this occasion he terrified her by asking her at discussion time for her opinion of the relationship between the characters Tom and Lydia in Lawrence's book *The Rainbow*. She cringed from attention. She was a person unused to having her opinions sought out. But Simon repeated his question and although his voice was gentle she recognized an insistence about it that couldn't be ignored.

Gazing down at the patch of floor in front of her feet, she cleared her throat and said, "Do you think that perhaps Lydia. . . ."

"Don't worry about what I think, Ann. It's what you think that matters. Just tell me honestly what you feel."

She kept her eyes down. "I feel that Lydia has a strong sensual attraction to Tom but at the same time she remains spiritually removed."

"Very good. Very good indeed. That's a very interesting point. . . ."

Gratitude obsessed her, almost blotting out the rest of the discussion. Her secret happiness lasted until coffee time when it was swamped by nervousness at finding the tutor by her side. He took a sip of coffee then smiled down at her. Again she felt acutely disturbed but she managed to smile in return.

"You must contribute more often to the discussions, Ann."

"Oh, no."

"Why not?"

"I'm too stupid."

"Stupid?" He stared at her. "Why on earth should you say that?"

He touched her arm. It was only for a second but it seemed to her to convey a special kind of sympathy and reassurance.

"You're a very sensitive and intelligent woman."

She was glad that some of the others interrupted at this point and she was able to drift away to tag on to another goup further along the corridor.

She felt secretly distressed to the point of tears. So strung-up did she feel she had difficulty in concentrating on the second part of Simon's lecture. Nevertheless, at discussion time she blurted out her thoughts on the conflict between Lawrence's sensuality and intellect. As she spoke she suffered a mixture of delicious excitement and bleak depression. She feared that Simon would despise her for talking nonsense.

It amazed her when he listened with respect. He even asked her a few thoughtful questions, as if he was the one who was learning something. The discussion developed into quite a lively one with

59

everyone joining in. She became so carried away she found herself talking out as much as, if not more than, the rest. So over-stimulated did she become, in fact, that she was glad to escape by herself immediately the meeting was over.

As she walked through the streets on her way home her mind raced ahead of her. New doors of understanding opened up as she thought of different points raised in Simon's lecture. Problems were tentatively worked out. Questions answered and new questions raised. She found it both fascinating and overwhelming to realize that the more she learned the more she realized how ignorant she was. It seemed that life would never be long enough now to find out all she wanted to know. But it gave such a stimulating purpose to living.

She began to talk freely in class discussion. Not so much in reckless bursts of nervous excitement but slowly, thoughtfully. She was still nervous and unsure of herself but she couldn't help enjoying the challenge of trying to think things through in her mind. She would give an opinion — perhaps quite a simple statement like, "I enjoyed that story."

Then Simon would nonplus her by saying, "Why?"

To have enjoyed the story and said so had seemed enough. The question having been put to her and in such an earnest way however, and as if her answer would be of interest and value, forced her to grapple with her thoughts.

"Isn't the purpose of a work of art to please?" she'd said. "Isn't it enough that I had an emotional reaction to the story? It pleased me. I liked it."

"Yes, but why did it please you? Why did it give you that particular emotional reaction?"

She felt her brain creaking as she forced open unused doors. It was almost painful. Out of some opening came blatant illogicalities. Gradually she began to recognize them as such before Simon had the chance to correct her. She would laugh and say, "Now I'm being illogical again." And she would retrace her steps and work out for her own satisfaction the line of argument or points of view she wanted to put forward.

A couple of times Simon and a group of the students, including herself, continued their discussions at the university club over a few drinks and a cheese sandwich.

She bought herself a new wool dress, a pair of high-heeled shoes and had her hair expensively cut and colour rinsed to accentuate its warmer burnished tones.

It was dark now before five o'clock and as often as not it was either raining or snowing and Simon insisted on giving her a lift home.

It was strange to be alone with him. After all the talk in the class

60

and at the club, they were both quiet. Yet there was an awareness in the car that spoke louder than words. At Canal Lane he stopped and turned towards her as she smiled and said, "Thank you for the lift. It was very kind of you. I hope it hasn't taken you too much out of your way. See you next week at the class."

To her astonishment and dismay he leaned forward and kissed her on the mouth.

"Goodnight, Ann."

She did not know how she got out of the car. But she heard it drive away as she entered the building and climbed the draughty stairs. Her mind was fevered by all sorts of strange emotions but it was still able to register the fact that it was her turn to wash the stairs, never a pleasant prospect on a wet winter's evening.

Later, when Charlie came home from work, guilt made her extra nice to him. She kissed him warmly in welcome and said wasn't it an awful day, knowing he liked a good grumble. She cooked beef, onions, carrots and potatoes for his dinner, followed by a rice pudding baked with lots of milk and sugar. It even had a dark brown skin on top exactly the way his mother used to make it.

Charlie supped it up and scraped his plate, and scraped it and scraped it until her nerves began to tense under the strain. But she managed to say in quite a calm voice, "I'm glad you enjoyed it, dear."

He stretched and smacked his ample belly with both palms. "Yes, that was good. And there's a good night on telly as well."

"Charlie, how about us going out for a change?"

"But it's a good night on telly."

"Well, tomorrow night then.'

"Why, is there a good picture on somewhere?"

"I wasn't thinking of going to the cinema."

"Out for a meal?"

"That would be nice too, but I was actually thinking of something more stimulating we could do together."

He laughed. "We don't need to go outside for that."

"Charlie!"

She got up from the table and went over to sit on the settee. Still laughing but in a lower, more growling key, Charlie came over and grabbed her in his muscular arms.

"I'm still game to do it in front of the telly. But you'll have to wait —" his attention began wandering away at the sound of the theme music of "Coronation Street" — "until the commercials are on."

Chapter Fourteen

"I'LL MISS the class over the Christmas holidays," she told Simon. "But Merry Christmas and Happy New Year to you when it comes."

"Don't rush away. I'll give you a lift home."

"No, thank you. The shops are open late tonight and I want to buy a few last-minute presents. Goodbye. . . ."

"Wait! I want to talk to you."

She didn't turn round but her steps faltered uncertainly. His long legs reached her before she managed to leave.

"I'm having a party at my flat on the twenty-seventh. I'd like you to come."

"Oh . . . I don't think. . . ."

"We'd get a chance to talk." His smile had the appeal of a little boy. "Say you'll come."

She smiled in return. "Yes, all right."

He wrote his address on a piece of paper and gave it to her but made no attempt to follow her further. She emerged from the fluorescent-lit building to the dark street with a sense of shock.

A cold wind was blustering along and she had to turn up the collar of her coat and hold down the skirts of it to protect herself. Even so, she shivered.

Charlie was meeting her straight from work at Boots Corner in Argyle Street. She caught a bus into town and sat staring at her reflection in the window. Even though her hair had been blown about, its professional cut had assured its return to a neat smart shape. Her thin face was saved by good bone-structure and large dark eyes.

But she was aware only of the anxiety in the eyes and the threads of lines etched on either side of them.

Charlie would have to find a parking place for the car. Instead of going straight to the multi-storey indoor car-park where there was usually plenty of room, he would be driving round and round the town bemoaning the lack of parking space. She dreaded being trapped in the car with him at a time like that. At best it was exhausting and she was glad on this occasion to have escaped the ordeal. She arrived at Boots first and stood back against the window to avoid being jostled by the passing crowds. Snowflakes began to swirl in the wind. They shimmered around the street lamps, flecked the dark sky and settled on people's hair and shoulders like cotton wool. Further along Argyle Street at the pedestrian precinct the Salvation Army band had formed a circle and launched into "Still the Night, Holy the Night". Some people had been forced by their children to stop and listen and look. Above the heads of the milling throng, multi-coloured reindeers pulling sleighs piled high with toys twinkled out and in, shaped by the myriad of fairy lights strung all along the street from one side to the other.

The music, the lights, the snowflakes affected her deeply, making her feel it was good to be alive.

"I left in plenty of time," Charlie puffed towards her, obviously upset at keeping her waiting.

"It's all right. You're not late. I'm early."

"Well, you shouldn't have been early. It's neither safe, nor decent for a woman to hang about a street corner on her own. You could have been molested."

Touched at his concern she took his arm. He kept talking as they joined the crowd bustling along.

"And that's the last time I'll let you persuade me to bring the car in. I've been wasting petrol driving around in circles trying to find a parking place. It makes me sick. Some folk are so selfish you'd hardly credit it. The way they park they either use up two parking places and you can't get in, or they box you in so tight you can't get out. They ought to be put up against a wall and shot."

"Well, never mind, you've got one now."

"It's easy enough for you to talk. You haven't the worry of trying to park the car. All you do is sit back and enjoy me chauffeuring you around."

"Where are we going first?"

"Across to the Poly." Lewis's department store had apparently, a lifetime ago, been known as the Polytechnic but she had never heard anyone except Charlie refer to it as such.

"How about a pair of warm pyjamas for your father?" she said as they entered the shop.

"I suppose so."

They moved at a snail's pace, jammed in among a solid mass of people.

"Hang on to me," Charlie said as they struggled to get on to the escalator. Then, later, after they'd bought the pyjamas for Grandpa Sommerville, slippers for Aunty Bella and a few stocking-fillers for nieces and nephews, he announced, "Come on down to the basement café and I'll treat you to something to eat. It'll save you cooking anything when you get home."

"Thanks, dear."

The heat and the crowds were making her feel sick and she was truly grateful for a cup of tea, although the self-service café was also hot and not only crowded but noisy. Dishes clattered ceaselessly over the rabble of voices and, above it all, the tannoy bellowed bargain offers from one department after another.

"What do you fancy?" Charlie asked. "Hamburgers and chips, ham and egg or fish and chips?"

"Just a cup of tea would do me."

"Don't be daft. I'm treating you to your tea. Make the most of it. Have whatever you fancy."

She had developed a headache. People in the queue were shouldering her along. In harassment she said, "Oh, all right, fish."

After crushing towards an empty table somehow carrying their trays as well as parcels they flopped down and Charlie gasped, "Thank goodness Christmas only comes once a year. I must have spent a fortune already. Don't just sit there like an accident looking for somewhere to happen. Eat up your fish and chips."

Using only her fork she separated a piece of fish and conveyed it daintily to her mouth while Charlie got stuck in with energy and enthusiasm.

"Here, Annie," he burst out while still chewing, "have we got enough grub in for our Christmas dinner?"

"We got all that out of the supermarket."

"But are you sure we got enough? Remember, there'll be — how many? — Pop, Aunty Bella, Fred, Isa and the kids, Helen and Dave, you and me."

"Charlie, I've been cooking Christmas dinner for all of them and ourselves for years. The only extra one this year is Dave."

"Well, that'll mean . . ."

"There's more than enough for everybody."

Charlie moaned and complained about Christmas but she could see in actual fact he looked forward to it with barely concealed excitement. Of course the television was always good.

She liked to have everything well-planned in advance and as usual she peeled the potatoes and prepared the vegetables, the cranberry sauce and the chestnuts on Christmas Eve. After icing the Christmas cake she even set the table, not forgetting the red candles, the centrepiece of Santa and his sledge, and the emerald green, lemon, yellow and crimson crackers with the silver bands. While she did this, Charlie, balanced on the wooden step-ladder, put up the paper decorations. He kept shouting to her to come and hand him up a bell or another strand of tinsel until she eventually protested in exasperation, "Why is it you always need me as a labourer, Charlie? Can you not even do a job by yourself?"

"Oh, if that's how you feel, I won't bother. I'll take the whole lot down again. It's just a lot of silly nonsense anyway. We just put it up to take it all down again in a few days. It's the same with all these cards. They're nothing but dust collectors. And just think of all the money that's been wasted. . . ."

She left the room quickly, bathed in sweat, in terror that she was going to have a fit of hysterics again. She could no longer be sure of what she would do or what might happen to her.

Chapter Fifteen

SHE'D ANNOUNCED quite casually during their Christmas Day celebrations that she would be going to another party in a couple of days' time.

"Eh? What party?" Charlie asked.

"My Literary Appreciation class party. The tutor's giving it."

Grandpa Sommerville said, "What's she saying?"

"She's gone back to school, Pop." Charlie shouted in the old man's ear.

"Crivvens! At her age?"

"I tell you, she's daft!"

"What's he saying?" Grandpa asked Aunty Bella.

"Annie's daft!"

"Not a bad lassie though. Why does her mother not talk to her?"

"Oh, it's a long story."

"What's she saying?" he asked Fred and Fred leaned over to yell in his ear. "Aunty Bella says you're a drunken old rascal!"

Isa screeched with hilarity and her sons rolled on the floor in stitches and wrestled each other in uncontrollable exuberance.

Charlie hadn't mentioned the party afterwards. It was obvious he'd forgotten all about it because when, a couple of days later, instead of settling down beside him to watch television, she began to put on fresh make-up and change her clothes, he was astonished. "What do you think you're doing?"

"Getting ready for the party."

"What party?"

"I told you, Charlie."

"You did nothing of the kind."

"The Literary Appreciation class party."

His surprise crumbled into uncertainty. "What kind of thing is it?"

"I don't know. Just an ordinary Christmas party, I suppose."

"I don't like you mixing with the Uni crowd."

"Why not?"

"You'll be getting yourself into trouble."

She couldn't help laughing. "What trouble, Charlie?"

"There's drug-taking and . . . and all sorts of queer goings on. They're a bad crowd up there."

Impulsively she kissed him. "Nonsense! It's just a lot of ordinary respectable folk like ourselves at the class. I don't know where you get your ideas about the university, Charlie. Do I look all right? Do you like my new dress? Isn't the band of embroidery round the neck and hem unusual?"

"You look like a Russian. You're not going to a party in boots are you?"

"It's cold outside."

"You'd better take your slippers in your bag."

"No, I don't think so."

"Why not? What's wrong with your slippers? I gave you these slippers for your birthday and you hardly ever wear them."

"I'd better go now."

"Just you watch yourself."

"Yes, dear." She kissed him again. "Cheerio."

The light on the landing was lit but its puny beam did nothing to cheer the maroon walls and damp stone stairs. In the tunnel of the entrance snow made horseshoe patterns where it had stuck to someone's heels as they entered.

Outside, a thick covering of white quietened the lane. Quickening her steps she turned the corner on to Dumbarton Road then crossed over and made her way up Byres Road towards Hilton Gardens. The tenement buildings there were old like those in Canal Lane but that was where the comparison ended. She could see by the amount of large windows on either side of the entrance that the flats must be very much bigger than the one she lived in. Peering at nameplates she found a copper one with "Simon Edgington" printed in black. After taking a deep breath she pulled the bell. She heard its muffled echo. Then there was a long silence. It suspended her in uncertainty. Had she got the day wrong? Or had he forgotten that he'd invited her, changed his mind about having a party and just gone out? No sound of a party, no sound of anything at all reached her, even when she pushed her ear furtively close to the door. Feeling miserable and foolish she made to leave. Then it occurred to her that she would feel even more foolish if she left and later found out that Simon had been in the loo and just hadn't heard the bell or he and the rest of the guests could be chatting in a far away room with the door shut. After all, she had only given one quick pull. She pulled it again.

This time she thought she heard a leisurely scuffling sound. The sound came nearer. Then the door opened to reveal a small woman with grey tufty hair. The woman said, "Christ!"

Ann's eyes wrinkled with anxiety. "Have I come on the wrong night or something? Simon invited me to a party. I thought he said tonight but. . . ."

"Come in."

She followed the dumpy figure in the loose top and baggy trousers through a book-lined hall as big as Canal Lane, and into a lofty-ceilinged room.

"I'm Mabel. Make yourself at home. Just clear a chair. Push some of these papers on to the floor, I was supposed to have this place all tidied and ready." She gave what sounded like a laugh. "Now I'll cop it."

"Am I the first then? Am I too early? It's after half-past seven."

"My God, what kind of parties do you give?"

"We don't give many parties — only at Christmas and Helen's birthday."

She supposed Mabel must be Simon's mother. Yet despite the grey hair and unmade up face, there was something about the smoothness of her skin and the straightness of her back that suggested a much younger woman.

"Where is Simon?"

Mabel lifted a cushion from the floor and tossed it on to the settee.

"He's either in the bathroom tarting himself up or he's gone out for the booze."

"Are you. . . ." She hesitated.

"I'm Simon's wife."

"His wife?"

"You look shocked. Didn't you know he was married?"

"No. Not that it matters, of course."

"I see."

"What I mean is . . ." She felt herself become red-faced and enormous-eyed. "He's just my tutor. It's not as if . . . I mean, I'm married too."

"I see."

"Look, maybe I'd better go. I've obviously come at an awkward time."

"Simon wouldn't like it if you left."

"Nevertheless, I feel. . . ."

"The kids are out at their Gran's. I've just to tidy up a bit, you can help if you like. It's not that I worry about the house but Simon's fussy. Especially if people are coming."

She could imagine how embarrassed, perhaps even angry, he would be to find that she had seen his sitting-room in such a mess.

"All right."

She began gathering papers and notebooks together. "Are these Simon's? Where should they go?"

"Christ, no. These belong to the kids. Simon's papers are all filed away. None of us would dare touch them. He has an office room at the back. There's never a pencil out of place through there.

Come on, I'll let you see it."

"Maybe we should get this place cleared first. Haven't the children got a desk or a place to keep their papers?"

"The bedroom on the right when you go out of here. What's that package you've brought? Is it a prezzy for Simon?"

"It's just a box of chocolates. You know how you should always bring something when you visit somebody's house for the first time."

"Oh? I never bother."

"Here, you have them."

"Thanks."

As Mabel unwrapped the chocolates and selected one, Ann attacked the books and papers strewn about. At running pace she reached the first bedroom and elbowed her way in. Her instinct was to put everything tidily away but she felt that time was at a premium and instead heaved everything on to one of the unmade beds.

Back in the sitting-room Mabel was hunkered down in front of the fire dreamily poking it.

"If you bring me your Hoover I'll whip round this place in no time. And a duster. Have you food or anything to prepare?"

"I thought I might make a few sandwiches later on. There's plenty of crisps and nuts to have with the drinks."

"Where's your kitchen?"

"Come on through. Make yourself at home."

Ann looked sharply at the other woman. She thought she'd detected a note of sarcasm.

In the kitchen she found its untidy confusion an agony. She had never realized before how much she needed some sense of order. Her fingers itched to organize the contents of innumerable paper bags into neatly labelled jars or canisters.

"Where's your Hoover? Oh, there it is. Gosh, I don't know how you can keep so calm, Mabel — with people coming and so much to do. I'll race through and see to the room if you want to stay here and put the crisps and nuts into dishes. Have you got glasses ready?"

Mabel laughed. "What's your name?"

"Oh, I'm sorry. I didn't introduce myself. Ann Sommerville."

She put a hand out while still clutching awkwardly at the Hoover, a feather duster and a wet cloth.

"Yes, I thought you might be Ann. Simon has told me about you."

"Oh?" She avoided Mabel's eyes. "Well, I'd better hurry with this if I'm going to get it done."

First she whipped round all the surfaces with the feather duster, wiping sticky patches with the wet cloth when necessary. Next she plumped up the cushions, tidied the curtain straight then attacked the carpet. She had worked her way to the door when a cold voice behind her said:

"What are you doing?"

"I've just finished. I'll put this away."

"Did my wife ask you to . . .?"

"No, no!" Ann raised a hot, pink face. "Oh no, I insisted. I was ridiculously early, you see. I was embarrassed and didn't want to be in the way. So while Mabel was doing something in the kitchen I said I'd Hoover in here. I insisted. I hope you don't mind."

He gave her a cautious sideways glance. "I'll pour you a drink. What would you like? I have whisky, gin, vodka. . . ."

"Gin and bitter lemon, please. I'll put this away. I won't be a minute."

In the kitchen Mabel was arranging roses in a vase with a kind of defiant bounce to her fingers.

"How's that?" she asked stepping back and gazing at her handiwork.

"They're beautiful."

"Simon bought them."

"What a lovely thought!"

"Oh, they're not for me. They're to make the room look pretty for you . . ." she paused for a second, "and the others."

She presented the vase to Ann.

"Oh, my love's like a red, red rose,
That's newly sprung in June;
Oh, my love's like a melodie
That's sweetly played in tune.
As fair art thou my bonnie lass . . . ."

"I'll take them through," Ann interrupted in an agitation of embarrassment.

Never in her life before had she met such a strange couple. She didn't know what to make of them.

Chapter Sixteen

"I TOLD him to piss off."

Zoë's voice had a drunken slur to it. Her mouth drooped loose and although she was sitting on the floor she swayed and flopped about. Her blonde hair slithered forward. She bunched it back with one hand. "Piss off, I said. You bastard."

Ann's shock was cushioned to some extent by the drink she had consumed herself. Nevertheless, she experienced a flutter of

69

distress. Her mind beat about in an attempt to escape. But astonishment kept dragging her attention back again.

Everyone in the room was on the staff of the university except Mabel and herself. Not one of the other students from Simon's extra-mural class was present. She didn't know whether to feel complimented or suspicious. Nobody in particular was listening to Zoë, but she continued, "Soddin' Gerry Paterson. 'What do you think I am?' I said. 'Piss off!' I said. 'You bastard.'"

The bearded man called over to Simon who was at the sideboard attending to the drinks, "Isn't Gerry coming tonight?"

"He'll wander in later."

Mabel said, "The last I heard from Gerry he was laying two. One he said was good in bed but not terribly intelligent. The other was intelligent but lousy in bed."

A woman sitting cross-legged on the settee said, "Trixy was the one who was lousy in bed."

"I always knew she was intelligent."

Ann switched her attention to Simon when he came over and asked if he could fill her glass.

She clung to it. "No, thank you. I've had more than enough."

"Would you like to see where I write my poems and stories?"

She nodded and followed him from the room.

"I'm working on a poem at the moment," he told her.

"I read your last volume of poetry. I thought it was marvellous."

He smiled down at her. "Here is my study."

He switched on the light to reveal a large square room with a flat-topped desk in the centre, and broad shelves up to chest level all around the walls. Everything was in perfect order. Even pencils and pens stood together in neat rows. Simon showed her many expensive-looking gadgets. There was tape-recording equipment, radio and stereo, a copying machine, a typewriter. But it was his filing system that really fascinated her.

"You've obviously put a great deal of thought and care into this. How long did. . ."

He was standing behind her and suddenly his arms slid round the front of her waist and his lips nuzzled the curve of her neck. She wriggled away and stumbled to one side, unsteady on her feet after two or three gins.

"You mustn't do that!"

"Why?" He smiled. "Don't you like it?"

"Yes, but. . ."

"What's wrong?"

"You're married and I'm married. That's what's wrong."

"My dear Ann," cupping her hand against his mouth, he kissed her palm. "What harm does it do my wife or your husband if we enjoy a pleasant flirtation?"

Again he bent his head over her hand. Gazing at his dark hair a tenderness rose in her like a pain. And when he took her into his arms for a few minutes she allowed herself the luxury of his kisses and caresses. Until gentleness changed to shared passion making her struggle free. She clutched at the shelves not sure if it was the drink or Simon's kisses that were making her feel so dizzy.

"I want to go home."

"It's early yet."

"It's not early. It's after midnight. That's late for me."

He sighed. "Must you go?"

"I want to go home."

"What are you two up to?" Mabel said from the doorway. Her grey hair looked as if she'd cut it herself and her voluminous bottle green smock did nothing to flatter her appearance. She was nursing a drink and trying to look nonchalant.

Simon said, "I'm taking Ann home."

"What's all the rush? Has her house caught fire?"

"My husband will be worried about me. I've never been out by myself this late before."

"It's only half-past twelve."

"I really must go. I'm sorry."

"I'll get your coat and handbag," Simon said.

"A proper little Cinderella."

Ann stared miserably at the other woman until Mabel smiled at her.

"Not to worry, there's worse things between heaven and hell."

"Thank you for the party. I hope I'll meet you again some time."

Mabel took a mouthful of whisky. "You will. You can bank on it." Then she sauntered away.

"Here you are." Simon held out Ann's coat and she allowed him to assist her into it.

"I'll just say goodbye to the others first."

He waited at the front door at the other end of the hall while she went into the sitting-room.

"I'm away, everyone. It was nice meeting you. Goodnight."

No one paid the slightest attention except one man who vaguely raised his glass in her direction.

"You're very quiet," Simon said once the car pulled away from Hilton Gardens.

"Why did you invite me?"

"Why do you think?"

"That's not answering my question."

"Dear Ann. You like asking questions, don't you? You ask more questions than that whole extra-mural class put together."

She was taken aback and ashamed. "I'm terribly sorry. I didn't realize. . . ."

"No, don't be sorry. You've more intelligence than all the rest of them put together."

"Oh, you can't mean that."

"I always say what I mean."

She smiled, "I'm not so sure about that."

"Why should you doubt me?"

She didn't answer and he went on: "I'll tell you why. It's because you doubt yourself."

She gazed at his hands, firm and confident on the wheel yet long-boned and sensitive-looking. After a time she said, "You still haven't told me why you invited me."

"My dear, it's perfectly obvious I would have thought. You're an attractive, intelligent woman. I enjoy speaking to you. I enjoy being with you."

They had arrived at Canal Lane and he stopped the car and turned towards her, sliding his arm along the back of her seat.

"I want to touch you and hold you. . . ."

It amazed her how his words triggered the muscles of her chest into losing their smooth rhythm. She had to struggle for control of her breathing.

"Goodnight, Simon. Thank you for a most interesting evening."

"Goodnight, my dear," he said.

She tried to tread softly through the entrance and up the stairs in case she wakened any of the neighbours. Then before she slid her key in the door she took several calming breaths. The house was dark and silent. Yet there was about it a sulky accusation that made her feel guilty and depressed. She slipped into the bathroom to clean off her make-up before risking the bedroom. There, she didn't dare put on the light. But even as she undressed in the dark she knew that Charlie was awake and that he had been worried about her. She decided however that it would be safer not to let on. But as she crept into bed Charlie obviously couldn't bear the silence any longer.

"What time do you think this is to come home?"

"I came away before the party finished."

"It's one o'clock in the morning."

"I thought you'd be asleep."

"I've been worried sick."

"I'm sorry."

"A fat lot of good you being sorry is going to do me now."

"Charlie, what more can I say?"

"That crowd up there can loaf about in bed all day tomorrow but I've to get up early for my work."

72

"All right, let's go to sleep now."

"Yes, you'll go to sleep easy enough. I can smell the drink off you from here."

"I'm not drunk."

"It's a disgrace. You're giving me a right showing up."

"Just go to sleep, Charlie."

"Going out at night on your own. You'll be the talk of the place."

"Charlie, I'm tired."

"It's not my fault you're tired. You could have been sitting here with me watching telly then going to bed at a decent hour."

"Yes, Charlie."

"What were you doing at this party anyway?"

"Talking."

"Talking?"

"Just talking."

"What could you possibly get to talk about for six hours?"

"Well, I'll tell you one thing, Charlie, I didn't talk about the telly."

"What's that supposed to mean?"

"Nothing. For pity's sake go to sleep. You'll never be able to get up in the morning at this rate."

"I heard a car. Who brought you home?"

"Charlie!"

"I've a right to know."

"My tutor."

"Your tutor!"

"Why the sneer?"

"What's he seeing you home for?"

"Common courtesy, perhaps?"

"You must think I'm daft."

"I think you're daft to be nagging on like this in the middle of the night instead of getting to sleep."

"I don't like these guys. And neither should you. I'm warning you, Annie. . . ."

"Oh, for Christ's sake, shut up!" she shouted.

He switched on the light and lifted a grey shocked face from his pillow.

"That's maybe the way your so-called clever friends talk but I'm having no bad language in this house. I keep a clean tongue and I'll thank you to do the same. It's about time you curbed that temper. That bad temper of yours will be getting you into trouble yet. There's always been a bad bit about you. . . ."

Turning away from him she pulled the bedclothes high over her head.

73

Chapter Seventeen

SHE DREAMED of Simon. In the dream they made love and she awoke feeling wet and swollen. Even her breasts ached and tingled as if his tongue had been caressing them. She cupped them in her hands under the blankets. She could hear the kitchen floorboards, then the lobby creak under Charlie's weight before he entered the room carrying a cup of tea.

"Here," he growled. "Don't say I'm not good to you."

His braces were dangling loose but his Aertex vest strained as a drum over his belly. He hadn't yet shaved and the grey stubble on his jowls bristled like the hair on his head.

"How do you feel?" she asked, struggling into a sitting position.

"Lousy."

"We'll go to bed early tonight."

"How I'm going to get through my work today I don't know."

"I'll get up and make you a good sustaining breakfast while you're in the bathroom getting washed and shaved."

"That's all I need — you in my way."

"I wouldn't be in your way if you're in the bathroom."

Gulping down a mouthful of tea she made to throw back the bedclothes. "It won't take me long to fry a bit of bacon and egg and it'll do you good."

"You stay where you are. I've told you before I don't want you messing about through there in the morning. I've my own routine to get me out to work of a morning and I don't want you messing it about."

Her burst of eagerness subsided. "Oh, all right. Have it your own way."

"It's not a case of having it my own way," Charlie protested indignantly. "If I had my way I'd be enjoying a lie back like you. I've got to go out to work and I take a pride in being regular. I've never been off a day, never even been late, not once in all the years. . . ."

"You'll be late today if you stand there much longer."

"See how you keep me back!" he shouted in harassment before hustling towards the bathroom.

She put her cup on the bedside table and slid back down in bed. Turning on her side she massaged her abdomen, moaning quietly as if she were in pain. Her fingers slithered down between her legs and immediately they found the moistness, her moans loudened as she felt an unexpected spasm of ecstasy. Then rolling over she buried her face against the pillow. She wept in shame and loneliness. Never before had she felt so utterly bereft. It took every

74

vestige of willpower to force herself up and drag herself through the day.

It was just before Charlie came home that the phone rang. She thought it would be Helen but even so, her lethargy persisted. She took her time in answering it.

"Hello."

"Hello, Ann." The cultured voice could only belong to one person. Immediately all her senses alerted. "How are you?" he asked. "None the worse for the party, I hope?"

"Oh, no. I'm fine, thank you. And you? And Mabel?"

"Mabel makes a point of never allowing anything to disturb her equilibrium."

"That's good."

"Not necessarily."

She kept silent, not knowing exactly what he meant. After a second he said, "Will you be in town tomorrow, by any chance?"

She paused before saying warily, "I might."

"Perhaps we could meet for coffee somewhere. I have to go in to buy some books.'"

"I must be home for my husband's lunch. That doesn't give me much time."

"If we made it somewhere convenient — like the Art Galleries perhaps?"

The chance of sharing a visit to the Art Galleries with someone so knowledgeable was too exciting to refuse.

"That would be lovely."

"Half-past ten?"

"Yes, all right."

"Until tomorrow then. . . ."

"Goodbye."

A surge of energy made her swirl around the lobby like a madwoman and when Charlie opened the front door she rushed at him and nearly bowled him over with the enthusiasm of her welcoming hug.

"Let go of me!" Charlie shouted but she could see he was pleased.

"Talk about a fruit and nut case!" He shook his head before plodding into the bathroom.

Singing to herself she dished the dinner and carried it through. She wanted to tell him. She wished she could tell him. But caution subdued eagerness and with the caution came guilt. There was no doubt in her mind that she had embarked on a slippery slope of secrecy and deceit. But her association with Simon Edgington had an unreal quality.

Sitting on the settee watching "Coronation Street" she knew she

75

belonged to a different world from his. She didn't believe her world and his world had met. Only occasional spurts of excitement made her wonder. Even up to the last moment before leaving for the Art Galleries next day, she did not believe it.

Despite the snow lying thick on the ground, she decided to walk. Her boots made crackling, crunchy noises as she strode along. Cold nipped through her gloves, numbing her fingers and making her breath stream out in icy clouds. Exhilarated by the tingle in her cheeks her steps quickened at the sight of the Art Galleries and University Park stretching out behind it and the university perched high on the hill.

Once at the entrance it occurred to her that she didn't know whether she was supposed to meet Simon outside or inside the building. There was no sign of him. Loitering about outside she soon began to shiver and had to stamp her feet and thump her gloved hands together in a desperate attempt to keep warm. In case he might be waiting inside she pushed through the revolving doors and gazed around the huge cathedral-like interior. Only a handful of people were wandering about. Another two or three were sitting at the coffee bar. Still no sign of Simon. She began to worry. Had he had been waiting at the coffee bar earlier and eventually thought she wasn't coming and gone through one of the archways to the rooms beyond? Or had he gone upstairs to have a look at the paintings? No use starting to search. The chances were she would keep missing him. It was such a huge place.

Would he be angry with her? Had he lost patience with her foolish confusion about their arrangement to meet? Had he just gone? She could have wept like a child with frustration and disappointment. No doubt the best thing to do now was to have a cup of coffee then to go home herself. Yet she didn't feel able to sit calmly drinking coffee. Restless, uncertain, unhappy, she glanced at her watch. Eleven o'clock.

Wandering aimlessly outside again the bitter cold shocked and depressed her. Everything now looked bleak and grey. An icy wind tugging at her skirts made her shudder. She felt chilled to her very soul. Yet still she couldn't tear herself away. She didn't know how long she had been standing by the time she saw Simon's tall figure striding towards her. The collar of his sheepskin coat was turned up and his hands were plunged deep into its fur-lined pockets. His briefcase was tucked under one arm.

He kissed her gently, tenderly on the lips. "I'm sorry I'm late." Then with a smile, "How are you?"

As he guided her back into the building she was at a loss for words. Anger at him for keeping her waiting, and then arriving in such a calm and charming manner as if nothing was amiss, tangled

76

with the astonishment she felt.

"Let's go to the restaurant upstairs," he was saying now. "That coffee bar is a plastic monstrosity."

"I thought it looked quite attractive. It's so modern and. . . ."

"Exactly. One would have thought they could have at least made an attempt to design something to fit in with the rest of the place."

On the way to the restaurant he drew her attention to various pieces of sculpture. He took his time strolling around the pieces, contemplating them from different angles. She followed his example although she still felt shivery and not very well and a vision of hot coffee kept distracting her.

In the restaurant he showed her the books he'd bought. They were mostly about Lawrence and they discussed him at some length (Simon, it turned out was doing a thesis on Lawrence for his Ph.D.).

"'I shall always be a priest of love'." Simon took a sip of coffee before adding, "Lawrence wrote that in a letter on Christmas Day 1912 soon after he'd completed his novel *Sons and Lovers.*"

"I doubt if the women in his life shared that view of him. He strikes me as being a very egotistical and selfish man."

"Why?"

"Well, for one thing he believed in giving way to his impulses. 'The truth of one's impulses' he called it, didn't he?"

"Is that necessarily selfish?'

"Yes. If we're reasonably civilized surely we must consider other people's feelings. He broke up a marriage because he wanted Frieda and afterwards Frieda wasn't even allowed to see her children. He wanted her body and soul. That's possessiveness not love."

"He believed in total commitment."

"Maybe so but it still seems to me to be suffocatingly possessive and restrictive. Sometimes I think I'm just against marriage altogether. It could be a case of the grass is always greener, but sometimes I look at single women and think how wonderful it must be to be absolutely free. Not to have to consider someone else's wants or needs or tastes. Not to feel guilty if one does something one wants to do oneself."

"It depends on the person one is married to. How much compatibility there is. So many things can go wrong. And not necessarily dramatic or positive things."

"Oh, no," she agreed. "They're not nearly so destructive as small negative wearing-away sorts of things."

· For the first time his grey eyes left her face and gazed instead at some point in the distance beyond her.

"Sometimes one partner can progress and develop and the other remain the same. An invisible gulf can begin to separate them as a result. This can be very sad."

She thought for a moment. "Yes, I know what you mean."

His attention strayed back to her face but there was a guarded expression in hes eyes now, a kind of wary, sideways look.

"Do you?"

But she had remembered Charlie, and a quick check with her watch made her cry out, "I'm late for Charlie's lunch. I'll have to run."

She rose and he rose too, feeling in his inside pocket for his wallet.

"I haven't the car with me."

"It's all right, I'll catch a bus. It isn't far. There's no need for you to rush. Thank you for the coffee, I enjoyed our talk."

"One moment," he said with the same quiet authority he used in the classroom.

She stopped in mid-flight to stare up at him. Slipping one hand round the back of her neck he drew her nearer. Then he kissed her slowly, tenderly on the mouth.

Chapter Eighteen

"HELLO, ANN."

"Oh, hello, Mabel!"

Bumping into Simon's wife in the Botanic Gardens, Ann tensed with guilt but quickly simulated a bouncy brightness. "It's nice to see you again. Are these your two daughters? Twins, no less, and beautiful ones at that!"

Mabel's face came to life with a glow of pride. The girls giggled together.

"Jane and Liza," their mother said, "this is Ann Sommerville."

"Hello," Ann said.

"They're doing so well at school I bought them these new coats as a special reward at Christmas."

"They look very stylish."

"Oh, they like to be stylish. Poor old Mum has to be content with clothes from Oxfam."

"The Oxfam shop in Byres Road? You're joking!"

"No, I'm not joking," Mabel said.

This explained the navy poncho, the too-wide, drooping neck of the maroon sweater and the other ill-fitting clothes.

"Is this the whole family?"

"No, that's Allan skipping on ahead and there's Billy. Billy's the eldest. I don't know where he's disappeared to. He's fifteen. It seems to be an awkward age. He used to be quite happy to fit in

78

with what the rest of us were doing but now he's gone all rebellious."

"They're a problem, aren't they? And a worry. And they get more so as they get older. My daughter's grown up and married and I still worry about her."

"Christ! And I've four kids to suffer."

The girls giggled again and Mabel said, "What are you doing at New Year?"

"Oh, we usually have a quiet time. Our next door neighbours come in just after midnight and we toast the New Year and watch the TV until one a.m. That's about all. The rest of the neighbours go further afield after that but we just go to bed."

"I meant New Year's Day."

"Nothing much."

"Why don't you come over to us."

"Oh, I couldn't leave my husband. Not on New Year's Day."

"I meant to bring him along. Bring your daughter and her husband too, if they're there."

"No, they're going to his relations for New Year."

"Well, you and your husband then. Come in the afternoon. Billy should be in then. I'd like you to meet him. He's a fine-looking boy and a good boy. When I said he was a bit rebellious I didn't mean he was a bad boy."

"No, of course not."

"In fact I've a feeling that he's going to be quite brilliant like his dad. Did you know Simon's aiming for a doctorate now?"

"Yes, you must be very proud of him, Mabel."

"Will you come on New Year's Day?"

"All right. Thank you. I'll look forward to it."

As she continued her walk through the snow-covered Botanic Gardens she wasn't sure if she looked forward to the visit or not. The more she thought about it the more unsure and worried she became. Charlie was even less enthusiastic, not to mention suspicious.

"Why does he keep dishing out invitations to you?"

"It's not him. It's his wife. I've got quite friendly with her."

"We've nothing in common with them. What do we want to go there for?"

"She was so insistent. I didn't like to keep refusing."

"My New Year's holiday will be wasted."

"You don't know that, Charlie. You might enjoy yourself. Simon and Mabel are very nice people."

"And the telly's always good on New Year's Day."

"Well, I'm sorry but I've promised we'll go."

"You know your trouble — you're downright selfish. It would

79

never have occurred to you to ask if I wanted to go first."

She laughed bitterly, incredulously. "When I think of all the times we've gone to Millport."

"What's Millport got to do with it?"

"Has it ever occurred to you to ask me if I want to go there?"

"Don't be stupid. You know you love your holiday at Millport. You look forward to it all year."

She bit her lip and looked away, realizing that if she allowed her emotions and her tongue full rein she could demolish the whole structure of their life together and the only relationship they had. But then what?

Folding into herself for protection she allowed Charlie's grumbles and accusations to flow over her head. On and on and on until they were actually in the car on their way to Hilton Gardens. It was then that she realized she had taken enough from him. She couldn't stand any more. Not another word.

She looked round at him. "All right," she said, "you win. Turn the car round and go back home if that's how you feel. There's no need for you to be a martyr. We'll just not turn up."

"We're nearly there."

"Oh, just turn the car and go home."

"I've got all dressed up and you've dragged me out. . . ."

"Charlie, why do you make me feel so continuously guilty? All our married life, every single day you've blamed me for something. You've made me out to be stupid, you've. . . ."

"You are stupid, that's why. You're always causing trouble. No wonder you had an accident the last time you drove a car. Your sister would be alive today if it hadn't been for your stupidity."

"Oh, Charlie!" A gigantic wave of tears threatened to engulf her.

"Here we are," he said stopping the car. "Just look at the place! These big flats are nothing but an eyesore. It's time they were knocked down. Look at that! That stonework's all needing pointing. And you would think with such a small patch of garden at the front they'd be able to keep it at least looking tidy. They just don't care, these Uni guys. All they're interested in is listening to the sound of their own voices."

She was sinking with horror inside.

"Well, don't just sit there." Charlie opened the door and nudged her towards it. "It was you who wanted to come. Let's get it over with."

She had to wait on the pavement with one hand on the car for support until Charlie locked up and came round beside her. She needed to take his arm before she was able to walk. It was as if she had not yet recovered from a long and debilitating illness.

"And don't you ever land me in anything like this again, do you

80

hear?" He had become more and more incensed and was now almost violent with rage. His arm was hard and unyielding and his tread so fast and aggressive her high heels tottered and she nearly twisted an ankle in her efforts to keep up with him.

The bell jarred through her head. Then, instead of either Mabel or Simon answering the door it opened to reveal a crowd of children who immediately blew back along the hall like leaves in the wind.

A man appeared from one of the rooms with a squealing toddler perched on his shoulders. Noticing them, the man shouted, "Come on in, folks, and shut the door, will you? It's hellish cold."

"Have I not seen you somewhere before?" Charlie said as they followed the man into a bedroom.

"Could be. Dump your coats on the bed. What's your local?"

"Bert's bar."

"It wasn't there then. I go the the Glenborough."

"I know!" Charlie shouted in sudden glee. "You're in the machine-shop."

"Good God, are you at Chrysler's?"

"Well, I'll be . . ." Charlie shook his head, relaxed and happy now. "What are you doing here then? I'm Charlie Sommerville, by the way. And this is the wife."

"Jack Bannerman. Pleased to meet you, Mrs Sommerville. This is one of my offspring, Denny we call him." He swung the child down onto the floor. "Away and torment your mammy. I'm one of Mabel's brothers. The whole clan's here. Come on through and meet them."

Ann was astonished at the crowd and the racket in the sitting-room. Innumerable children of all ages leapt and wrestled and raced around. Men and women sat in a big semi-circle in front of the fire talking, or rather shouting, to each other in their efforts to be heard above the din of the children. All that is, except Simon. He rose, smiling a welcome as soon as he caught sight of her. Yet there was a distant look about him as if he'd shut the whole place out and gone somewhere else in spirit.

He offered her his hand and said gently, "Happy New Year, Ann."

"Happy New Year, Simon. This is my husband Charlie. Charlie, this is Simon, my tutor."

"Happy New Year, Charlie."

"Happy New Year to you!" Charlie shouted jovially as he pumped Simon's hand up and down.

Other introductions were made and drinks poured. All the people present were brothers and sisters and nephews and nieces of Mabel. Her mother was also there, a small wiry woman with

81

knowledgeable eyes and a sharp voice that every now and again cut through the general rabble.

"It's time you fed the baby, Ella. Away and get its bottle made up. Jack, stop acting the fool and swinging Denny about like that. You'll make him sick. It's time you got some decent clothes, Mabel. You look a right frump."

Mabel was sitting placidly knitting. She laughed. "I'm no dolly bird, Mother. And I never will be. So why bother?"

"You could make the best of yourself. It's all a matter of money. Spend some on yourself for a change. That's a smart suit your wearing, Simon. That must have cost a pretty penny."

"I don't agree that it's all a matter of money, Mrs Bannerman," Simon said. "But I have told Mabel that it's no economy to buy cheap clothes."

"Words are cheap enough, Simon. But facts are facts, and there can't be much left for her to buy anything after you and the children are kitted out with the best that money can buy."

Jack bawled across the room, "Leave off, Mother. Give us a hand with Denny. He seems to have got something stuck in his throat."

The child was loudly hawking and choking.

Mrs Bannerman reached him in a few quick strides, thumped him on the back then grabbed him by the heels, whipped him upside down and thumped him again.

A sticky sweet shot from his mouth and stuck to the carpet. Denny began to scream indignantly. Mrs Bannerman righted him and proceeded to pace the floor, nursing him in her arms.

No one else in the room paid the slightest attention to the incident. One of the other men was enjoying a noisy wrestling match with two young boys. A woman was changing a baby's nappy, adding a foul stink to the general assault on the senses. Other women and men were laughing and talking together. Charlie was sitting back puffing at his pipe listening and making the occasional contribution.

"So you were one of the Brylcreem Boys," he shook his head at Dougal Bannerman. "I was more down to earth, lad. The good old RAs. I remember one time in the desert. . . ."

Ann's distress at Charlie's remark to her when they had first arrived had not only remained but intensified with the noise and confusion until she could bear it no more. She slipped unnoticed from the room then didn't know which way to turn. She tried the handle of the bathroom door and found it locked. She crossed the hall to go into one of the bedrooms but some children raced past her and tumbled screaming on to the beds. She just stood distractedly, helplessly, until a comforting arm went round her

82

shoulders. The next thing she knew she was in Simon's writing-room and sobbing uncontrollably against his chest.

Eventually she stopped weeping and moved back from him in embarrassment.

"I must look a sight. I'd better go and splash my face with cold water and put on fresh powder."

"Oh, Ann," he said.

"I'm sorry."

"Don't be sorry."

"I don't know what came over me."

"I find the clan somewhat overpowering myself. And you'll have noticed I'm not Mrs Bannerman's favourite son-in-law. She can't make me toe the line or pin me down and she hates me for it."

"You're so different from the others. I expect she just doesn't understand you."

"She understands that she can't rule me as she rules the others. Although I've never actually quarrelled with her. All the others have. They seem to enjoy fighting, and the noisier the better. They thrive on it even though they always lose and Mrs Bannerman always wins. Mabel is the quiet one in the family — compared with the others. I don't think she cares enough about anything to put up any kind of struggle for it."

"She cares about you and the children."

"She loves the children very much. Nevertheless she allows her mother to practically bring them up. That old woman has interfered so much with my children it doesn't bear thinking about. She'll do anything to get her own way, including bribing them with money, clothes, holidays . . . ." His voice had become bitter and his attention diverted to some point beyond her.

"It's a pity you live so close to her, Simon. Perhaps if you lived further away and Mabel was out of the sphere of her influence."

"I've tried everything — short of a shouting match. I refuse to become like them. I've guarded my privacy. I've been stern with my children. I've taken jobs as far away as Africa. Certainly Mabel has always come with me. But she's never happy away from her mother and her brothers and sisters and all their numerous offspring. She becomes more and more lethargic and depressed and I find it very difficult not to be affected by this and become seriously depressed myself. But as far as Mabel is concerned it always ends up by a telegram or a letter arriving to herald some crisis in the Bannerman family and off she runs back to them. She has never been a fully committed wife. But," he shrugged, "I have no wish to run Mabel down. She is a fine woman. She has many good qualities. I have much affection for her. I love her."

"I'm sure she loves you too," Ann said. "I've seen the way she looks at you. I'd better go and powder my face now. If you'll excuse me . . . ?"

His whole attention focused on her again. "Do you want to come back in here and sit in peace and quiet for a while?"

"No, Charlie might wonder where I've gone. It wasn't the noise anyway. I was feeling upset about something else before I arrived."

She meant to go but seemed to be attached to Simon by invisible threads. A delicate web, beautiful yet dangerous, spun around her as she stood gazing at him, until eventually he lifted her hand and lightly explored it with his lips.

Chapter Nineteen

BEFORE THE classes resumed after the Christmas and New Year holidays they met for a coffee in the Art Galleries and a walk in Kelvingrove Park. Again he was late. Again her indignation melted under the tenderness of his smile and his apparent pleasure at the sight of her. His eyes lit up with a mixture of surprise and childlike naïveté that was totally disarming in such a sophisticated man. She hadn't the heart to complain or to show resentment against him. Anyway, her pleasure matched his. It felt so good to see him and to be with him. On this occasion they had more time.

She had told Charlie she was going to have lunch with Zoë and had dug in her heels, refusing to be bullied out of her plan.

Over coffee she and Simon discussed his writing. She discovered it meant much more to him than teaching.

"Why do you prefer writing to teaching?" she asked him. "You're such a good teacher."

He smiled, "It's not because I believe like Shaw that those who can — do, and those who can't — teach. I believe we are all creative workers whether we are teachers, housewives, students, salesmen or businessmen."

"I'm sure I'm not very creative."

"Perhaps you have been so inhibited," he said gently, "that you don't know your true self. I think that to develop one's creativity one has to feel free, in spirit at least."

She laughed, not without a tinge of bitterness. "Oh, that explains it then."

"You feel inhibited," he prompted.

"It's just that Charlie's got this obsession with television. Sometimes I think I'll go mad at home. I just can't bear to sit night after night vegetating in front of that box. I feel I've such a lot to learn. It's terrible to waste so much time. At my age there isn't that much of it left."

Her burst of emotion left her trembling and Simon placed a hand on her arm and allowed it to wait there until she had calmed down.

"I know how you feel," he said after a minute or two. "One has to use one's powers, mind, feelings, sensibilities in the ways you want them to be most potent, most full of 'virtue' — in the original sense of the word. I always remember something I read by Addison. The exact words escape me but he said the mind (and all that implies) is like a garden. If you let one day go by without cultivation, the weeds grow."

"That I believe," she said. "That is so true! Oh, I wish Charlie would take some interest in other things, have a more positive, optimistic view. So much of his life — both of our lives — seem negative and hopeless. Often I feel like giving up. But mostly I keep wanting to try."

"Yes, one has to try to be responsive and alive and full of feelings. They don't just happen. Or, they happen less and less the older one gets. Keeping alive is difficult. It's tied up with getting older. And some of us get older quicker than others."

"Charlie's always telling me to act my age."

"Age has got nothing to do with it. It's the quickening one must continue to feel — at art, music, literature, sadness, poverty, one's mate. That's what's important."

She gazed across at him with large liquid eyes. It seemed to her, at that moment, as if he had appeared by magic when she was at the point of drowning, and offered her a lifebelt.

Suddenly he leaned across and kissed her.

Afterwards she said, "One thing we will be creating if we're not careful and that's a reputation — a bad one!"

"You worry about what people think?"

She thought for a moment. "It's the guilt I worry about."

"What guilt?"

She shrugged.

"Have we time for a look at some paintings? I don't know about you but I needn't be back for lunch today."

"Mabel expects me when she sees me. Why don't we have a look at everything? Then have lunch. Then have a walk in the park."

She laughed with happiness and excitement. "Oh, Simon, I'll treasure this day."

"Dear Ann," he said. "You're so alive and vital and responsive. You gladden me. You can't know how you shine a light into some of the dark places inside me."

They strolled around holding hands for a time sharing a companionable silence. Then Simon said, "Would you like to read the manuscript of the book I'm working on, Ann?"

"Is it another work of literary criticism?"

"No, it's my first attempt at a novel. I'd be interested to know what you think of it."

"I'd love to read it of course but I'm hardly qualified to criticize your work."

"It's your response as an intelligent reader that I'd value. I don't want an academic critique."

"All right."

Her eyes brimmed up with gratitude and she had to avert her gaze in case he might think her over-emotional and foolish. She kept a tight hold of his hand however. Only when they eventually came out on to the street did she pull her hand away from his and walk a little apart, stiff and self-conscious, like a stranger. The chances of meeting anyone she knew in the park on a cold winter's day were slim. But it was different on the main street. The change in her attitude reminded her of the illicit nature of their meetings. She had enjoyed his company and been grateful for it but now it occurred to her that she should give their relationship more serious consideration.

"I'll drop the manuscript into your flat tomorrow." His gaze melted towards her, "If that's all right with you?"

She replied with a carelessness she did not feel, "Fine. Come in time for coffee."

Afterwards she found her invitation and his acceptance of it too incredible and frightening to think about. She would be alone with him in the house. Charlie's house. If Charlie knew he would think she had invited Simon for only one thing. He would be outraged and he would despise her. Just as her mother despised her for wanting to be alone with Joel.

"I've tried to bring you up to be a clean-living Christian woman," her mother always said. "But you bring a foreign seaman in here and I shudder to think what filthy carry-on you get up to alone in that room with him. The shame and disgrace of your behaviour will be the death of me yet."

She experienced the fear and the guilt of her youth as acutely as if the clock had been suddenly turned back and she was only a girl again.

One part of her mind told her that it was her home and no one could or should object to her having a friend in for a cup of coffee. But the strongest part of her lost itself in the terrifying maze of her mother's rules of respectability.

To this day she could not bring herself to sew on a Sunday without the spectre of her mother's horror rearing up at her elbow.

"What'll people think? Come into the house at once (she had been sitting out in the garden) and put that sewing down, you wicked girl! No one's supposed to do any work on a Sunday. What would the minister think of us if he saw you?"

There had always been the anxiety of someone knowing, watching, seeing.

There had been so many rules, so many sins. She had been aching to burst free of them and had, she realized now, married the first man who had asked her because she imagined he would be the magic key to her freedom. In a home of her own she would be free. But she was no freer now than she had ever been. The chains were deep inside her.

Her mother's house was a grey semi-detached with ribbon of garden at the front and a drying green and vegatable patch at the back. It was in Cairnpark — the exclusive Council "scheme" as they used to call it. "Only those and such as those," her mother liked to boast, "qualify for a house in Cairnpark."

She remembered the fawn blinds at her mother's window with their cream fringes and tassels. They were always drawn exactly one-third down each window. No one except special visitors was allowed to use the front door and behind the back door there was a little rack for shoes with a folded newspaper under it to catch any dirt.

Her father worked in the garden a lot, more for the chance to smoke his pipe than anything else. Smoke was not allowed to desecrate the inside of the house.

The house sucked her into its intimidating centre. It was as if she had never left it and she waited for Simon with the same confusion of guilt and joy with which she waited for Joel.

"Just as I thought," Simon said when he arrived. He gazed around after giving her a friendly absentminded kiss. "You are well organized and you keep a clean and tidy house."

It seemed to give him immense satisfaction to examine his surroundings as he strolled through the hall and into the kitchen with Ann.

"The kettle's just about boiling," she said.

It was so strange to see him in her kitchen, slim and elegant in his light blue denim suit. He folded his arms and leaned back against the table still studying the place with interest. She noticed black hairs curling from the open neck of his denim jacket and from under the cuffs.

"It's more comfortable through in the living-room," she said, putting the coffee jug and a plate of biscuits on the tray that lay in readiness on the work surface next to the cooker.

He smiled and gave a little flick of one hand to indicate that she should lead the way.

"Is that your book?" She looked across at the parcel he'd laid beside him on the kitchen table.

"Yes. I'll bring it through with me."

As soon as she had poured the coffee and they were settled together on the settee she undid the wrappings and opened the cardboard file. At first she was taken aback by the crowded lines of writing, so small she doubted whether she'd ever be able to decipher it. After a few minutes, however, she found the key to his special brand of shorthand and with the aid of her glasses was able to read a few pages without too much difficulty.

Sipping his coffee, he watched her in silence.

"How much work have you still to do on it?" she asked.

"This is only the first draft. If you finish reading it by tomorrow afternoon come to Hilton Gardens and we can talk about it."

She nodded and laid it neatly aside so that she could drink her coffee.

The nearness of him on the settee excited her and she consciously began preening herself in an effort to excite him. She crossed her legs so that her slim thighs and legs were shown to best advantage. When she leaned forward to refill his coffee cup she hoped that he would notice the little bulge that showed at the neck of her button-through dress, the top button of which she had dared to leave undone before he arrived. She was in a fever of need for him to kiss and caress her but at the same time was keenly grateful that he did neither.

After he finished his coffee he rose and strolled over to look at the bookshelves in the corner.

"They were my father's," she explained. "My mother was going to put them out after he died."

"Scott, Stevenson, Defoe. . . ." Simon's long fingers gently caressed the spines of the books.

"He was a quiet man. I never really got to know him. Except that he liked reading and looking at paintings and playing the piano."

She remembered the piano at home, so highly polished that its dark surface reflected like a mirror. Her father never played it except occasionally in a wooden kind of way when the minister paid one of his visits. Then, he had to accompany the singing of a hymn. She might never have known that he could play anything else or in any other way, or have given any thought to whether he could or couldn't. But one day she had gone out shopping with her mother and Constance, and at the shops her mother had discovered that she'd forgotten her purse and sent her back to fetch it.

She would never forget coming up the garden path and hearing the haunting strains of Sibelius's *Valse Triste* swirling exquisitely from inside the house. It was like meeting her father for the first time and being shocked with the realisation that he was a stranger.

Simon glanced at his watch then smiled over at her, his eyes softening with tenderness and affection.

"I must go now. I have a lecture to give. I appreciate the trouble you're willing to go to over my manuscript. It's unfair of me to ask you to read it before it's typed. . . ."

"Not at all. I'm looking forward to it."

She went with him to the door, happiness soothing deep down into her very soul.

"Until tomorrow, then?" He bent down and kissed her gently on the lips.

She smiled her gratitude up at him, "Until tomorrow."

Chapter Twenty

SHE SET about the task of reading the first draft of Simon's book with great earnestness and dedication. Beside the manuscript she set a notepad and pencil and determined to jot down her spontaneous reactions to each page as she went along. Then later she would write a carefully considered criticism. She settled her reading glasses on her nose, tucked her hair behind her ear and immersed herself in the story. It was told from the viewpoint of Matt Roland who at the beginning of the book worked in the pay office of a nut, bolt and screw manufacturers. Ann suspected that Simon had modelled Matt on himself. Simon had once worked at a similar job and there was the feel of Simon in Matt's detached attitude to life and to his companions.

The more she read on, however, the more disturbed and uncertain she became. There was an implicit sense of superiority tinged with mockery in the fictitious character that jarred on her. The way his boredom and lack of interest in his job was expressed in lazy doodling and wherever possible in devious avoidance of his share of the work offended her Calvinistic sense of propriety. Even more than the lazy avoidance of work, though, it was Matt's attitude that shocked her. There were certain rules of right and wrong that she had taken for granted every decent person accepted. But far from feeling guilty or seeing anything wrong in his behaviour, Matt regarded his antics in deceiving his employers as a series of intellectual victories.

Resentment began to simmer at the back of her mind. It pushed up pictures of her father plodding back and forwards to his office job for a lifetime of devoted service. It was as if Matt had been in her father's office and caused her father extra work and worry.

It isn't fair, she thought bitterly every time Matt scored a dubious victory over his older office colleagues or viewed them with contempt. *My father was a good man.*

She had to keep reminding herself that Matt was only a character in a novel. He was not Simon and he had no connection with her father. But her sensible school-marm reminders were useless in freeing herself from the emotional spider's web in which she was becoming more and more entangled.

As the book progressed, Matt won a bursary to Cambridge and, while recognizing the writing skill that brought Cambridge so vividly to life for her, Ann's resentment increased to fury. Here was a young man blessed with intellect and with a chance to live and work in idyllic surroundings and enjoy every advantage that such a life could offer and what did he and the other undergraduates do? For most of the time, it seemed, they indulged in the most infantile pranks. Some of what they regarded as clever and splendid fun was downright dishonest and, had it been committed by apprentice joiners or plumbers, would have resulted in a term of imprisonment. Other antics were, in her opinion, either cruel or immoral or both. Everything was considered amusing or smart, except being nice and kindly. Indeed, these words were regarded as particularly stupid and contemptible.

There was a scene at a sherry party given by the Dean during which Matt and his friend Bunker ogled a beautiful girl. She joined them and remarked on how kind it was of the Dean and his wife to have given them such a nice party. This innocuous phrase damned the girl as stupid in Matt and Bunker's eyes and they mentally dismissed her as being of no further interest.

It was the kind of sentiment Ann would have expressed herself and she felt not only hurt and insulted at Matt and Bunker's attitude, she hated them. Trembling with fury she tossed down her pencil and went to make herself a cup of tea.

"Silly, immature, idiotic snobs!" Her voice trembled into the silence of the kitchen.

She hated the book and the intensity of her emotion dismayed and perplexed her. Even the love element came as a shock. She had expected women to be portrayed with romantic love and tenderness and found instead several sexual acts enjoyed as such with total concentration and absorption.

"Male chauvinist pig!" she said, not knowing if she meant Matt or Simon or both.

After finishing the manuscript she replaced it in its folder without including her notes. After reading them over she recognized their emotional content and was ashamed. This was not literary criticism. Then she thought, "To hell with literary criticism and all its stereotyped jargon. At least this is an honest response." And she pushed the notes into the folder.

90

While automatically preparing Charlie's lunch, she planned a few extra paragraphs giving her overall impressions of Simon's book. She struggled to be fair. There were many fine passages in it. Vivid word pictures lit up her mind. She could see in her imagination Matt and Bunker riding their bicycles against the backround of the college with gowns flapping merrily in the breeze as vividly as if she had seen them in reality.

Charlie didn't notice how abstracted she was. He belched appreciatively after eating his rolls and boiled ham then folded his *Daily News*.

"Time I was off!"

She raised her face for his kiss. He gave her a noisy one, adding, "See you at teatime."

The boards in the lobby creaked. The door banged. The small flat was suspended in silence again. She went straight to her notepad and wrote down the extra pragraphs before leaving for Simon's place.

He met her at the door with such naked pleasure and anticipation brightening his face, she became frightened at how critical some of her comments of his work had been.

Mabel was hovering with carefully affected nonchalance in the background.

"Hi."

"Hello, Mabel."

"What's that you're clutching so tenderly to your bosom? A prezzy for me? Or Simon?"

Ann was taken aback that Mabel didn't know.

"It's Simon's novel. He gave it to me to read."

Surprise rippled across the smooth pool of Mabel's face. "He's never let me read it."

"Come through to the writing-room, Ann." Simon eased the novel from her. "We can talk in peace there."

"I've just jotted down some initial reactions," she said worriedly.

"Good."

In his writing-room with all its electrical equipment and complicated filing systems he ushered her to a seat. Then he settled himself behind his desk and prepared to digest her notes. His brow was supported on his hand and it shaded his eyes so that she could not discern what reaction if any her words were having on him.

At last he looked up and there was a dignified coolness in his expression.

"Ann, you've made an elementary gaffe."

She stiffened defensively. "Oh?"

"I am not Matt."

"No, but you obviously modelled him on yourself."

91

"There's a lot of Matt in me; or a lot of me in Matt. But I include him. Please don't identify my reactions with Matt's. I do not despise niceness and kindness."

"I'm sorry. That element in the book made me so angry."

"You over-reacted."

"I wonder why."

He shrugged. "Your experience of life seems to me to be narrow. I'm not trying to diminish you. Your experience has been real and deep and intense. But it is restricted. What you miss is a width of experience with different social groups. You don't seem to know that other social groups have other standards, habits and moral attitudes."

"That doesn't mean that when I do come up against different standards, habits and moral attitudes either in real life or in books I should necessarily approve of them."

"What I'm saying is that your attitude and beliefs are very much determined by a pretty local area and people."

"So I hated Cambridge. So did D.H. Lawrence. Remember what he said about it? 'I went to Cambridge and hated it beyond expression.'"

"I didn't ask for an opinion on Cambridge, Ann, but on my novel."

She thought for a minute.

"Most of the novel was set in Cambridge and you have succeeded in giving a very vivid picture of it. That seems to me a measure of your good writing. I can see the place so clearly in my mind. What I'm really criticizing, I suppose, is the life you portrayed there."

"I portrayed life as it was."

"And people as they were?"

"Yes."

"You're saying that Matt and Bunker are typical of Cambridge undergraduates — how they think, talk and behave?"

Anger flashed to the surface again. "Well, if such stupid, infantile behaviour is typical, I certainly don't think much of it."

"The only question that matters is — is it a true portrayal? Art is a journey towards the truth."

"Yes, but, Simon, it's your truth. I mean, it's your way of looking at Cambridge. It's your way of looking at people. I got the impression that you were meaning me to admire Matt, identify sympathetically with his attitude to life and people."

"The reaction I have shown Matt to have is authentic but not necessarily comprehensive, and certainly not the only possible one. One should not automatically look only at people's good points; or look at them first. One should observe the world, and the people in it 'steadily and wholly'. See it all."

"Matt is so uncharitable. He doesn't see it all and it strikes me you don't either, Simon."

"It's afterwards that you can give your charity its head," Simon went on patiently but with a stiffness that contained disapproval. "Not in your thoughts necessarily, if charity is getting in the way of seeing the truth whole and steadily. But certainly in one's actions. And that's maybe the mistake you make about me (and Matt). My thoughts and observations may seem critical — yes, certainly, but I try to keep my actions charitable. But as a writer one can't let a pre-judgement of charity get in the way. Criticism of life and people is essential. How else does one know the good from the not-so-good and the downright rotten?"

She wasn't quite sure what he meant and suspected that he was only throwing up a smoke-screen of words with which to protect himself. She wanted to press the point about the book expressing his particular view of life, but she hadn't the heart. Nor could she bear to alienate herself further from him.

Instead she gazed anxiously at his closed face, "It was beautifully written," she said.

Chapter Twenty-One

AT THEIR next meeting Simon said, "I have to go through to Edinburgh soon. I've some people to see and a lecture to give. I thought I'd go early and have a look at some book shops. I'll stay overnight because I'll be going on to Aberdeen early next morning. Would you care to come with me?"

"To Aberdeen or to Edinburgh?"

"Both if you can manage it."

She stared at him worriedly. "Stay with you overnight, you mean?"

"I want to hold you and be tender with you and make love to you."

She didn't know what to say. It seemed incredible that a man like Simon could want her. At last she shook her head.

"Charlie would be suspicious, to say the least. No I couldn't get away. Not overnight."

For the first time she realized that she and Charlie had never been apart for one night in all their married life. Even when Helen had been born she hadn't left the marital bedroom. The midwife had come to the house.

"Come during the day then. Come with me to Edinburgh. We can leave early and you can be back in the evening before your husband returns from work."

She hesitated worriedly again. "I'll be seeing you at the class before that."

"Say you'll come."

His hands were deep in the pockets of his sheepskin coat. His collar was turned up against the blustering wind but strands of black hair strayed across his face making him crease up his eyes. It gave him a young and vulnerable look.

She tried to smile. "All right."

He didn't touch her or say anything, but he smiled in return.

Turning up her own coat collar she gazed around to see if a bus was coming. "I've got to go into town now." Eventually she spotted one approaching. "Here's a bus that will do. I'd better run, Simon. I'll see you at the class. Goodbye just now."

She touched him briefly, affectionately on the arm. Then after boarding the bus she turned to wave but he had strolled away without looking back.

The last thing she fancied doing was stuggling through crowds of shoppers, and she wasn't in the slightest interested in making any purchases. However, she managed to rally enough concentration to buy Charlie a pullover, a shirt and two pairs of socks, knowing that this would please him.

"How much did you say you got them for?" he asked. "Annie, you're miles away. What's up with you? You're dreamier than ever these days."

"What did you say?"

"How much were they?"

She told him.

Then he said, "Have you been up to anything?"

Startled, she focused all her attention on him.

"Up to anything?"

"That's what I said."

"I don't know what you mean."

"You look as if you've robbed a bank and you're expecting the police to knock at the door at any minute."

She tried to cover her distress with laughter. "No, I haven't robbed any bank. I'm just tired. It was a terrible crush in the shops."

That night she dreamt about Simon again.

She dreamt about him all the time now, restless, pasisonate, disturbed dreams that sometimes merged into nightmares. Even during waking hours her thoughts became obsessed and when one day the doorbell rang and she opened the door and found Mabel standing there she nearly fainted, believing for a crazy moment that Simon's wife had been able to read her mind.

Mabel said, "Poor Ann! There's no need to look so apprehensive.

94

I'm not going to eat you. Although I wouldn't say no to a cup of tea."

Mabel sauntered after her along the lobby and into the kitchen.

"Nice place you've got here. My God, not a crumb to be seen, not a dirty cup, not a thing out of place. How do you manage it?"

"I've only the one child and she's not a child any more, and she's not here."

For a horrible few seconds the unexpected urge to weep almost overcame her. She made the tea as quickly as possible and set the tray.

"Let's go through to the sitting-room. It's warmer." Then once they were settled at the fire, "Would you like to try one of these biscuits? They're home-made."

"I shouldn't," Mabel said. "I'm getting like a barrel. But what the hell!" She helped herself to two. "Aren't you having any?"

"No, I like to watch my figure."

"You like other people to watch it, you mean. Especially men-people."

"I hadn't really thought of it like that. At least. . . ." She paused worriedly. "I don't *think* I thought of it like that."

Mabel laughed. "Even if you had — so what? It wouldn't be the end of the earth. It's only human nature, duckie.'"

"I suppose it is. What I can't understand. . . ." She stopped in confusion.

"Yes? Well, come on. Tell me!"

"It's none of my business really. . . ."

"But?" Mabel prompted.

"Well, Simon is such an attractive man. . . ."

"Isn't he, though?"

"If I were in your shoes I'd be worrying myself sick about looking as attractive as I could all the time so that he wouldn't be tempted to look at anyone else. I'd do everything I possibly could. . . ."

"I told you before — I'm no dolly bird. Anyway, looks aren't all that important to Simon."

"Aren't they?"

"No. As long as he gets someone to adore him. Actually he's a very complex man. Do you mind if I take this bloody poncho off? Between that, the tea and your fire I'm getting roasted."

"I'm so sorry. I should have said. . . ."

Mabel had disappeared in a flurry of maroon tassels but soon emerged again somewhat breathless with hair standing on end. Giving her hands a quick rub over her head, she settled down and lifted her tea.

Ann stared at her.

"Forgive me, Mabel, but this is the first time I've seen you in something fitting. I mean, that sweater and those slacks show that you have a marvellous figure."

"A fat figure."

"Not fat, voluptuous perhaps. But that's sexy."

"My boobs are too big."

"I'm green with envy."

"You should have had more children, Ann."

"I don't know if I would have been able for the worry of more than the one. I'm an awful worrier, you know. I get so anxious about things. Mabel, do you mind me being a friend of Simon's? Yes, of course you do," she answered herself miserably. "I won't go back to the class. I won't see him again."

"Christ! Don't do that." Mabel suddenly alerted with distress. Fear flashed in her eyes. "I want you and Simon to be friends."

"But. . . ."

"I mean it."

"All right," Ann said staring at her in perplexity.

Mabel relaxed into her usual serene calmness and went on to explain that she had been passing and had remembered that Canal Lane was where Ann lived. "I just thought I'd be friendly and drop in."

"You're welcome any time."

"I bought some wool for a new sweater for Billy. You haven't met him, yet, have you? He had a last-minute invitation to a friend's party. I was going to try to make him stay for the family gathering but Simon said if he didn't want to stay I should let him go. He's a great believer in the freedom of the individual, is Simon. Mind if I have another biscuit?"

"Help yourself."

"At the same time he believes in total commitment. I've always felt there was a contradiction there."

"Oh, I don't know. In marriage, for instance, it could be that a person freely chooses to make a total commitment to his partner."

"In marriage it's usually the woman who is expected to 'freely choose to make a total commitment' — as you put it."

"Are you a women's libber?"

Mabel laughed. "I'm a proper little *hausfrau*. Haven't you noticed?"

"Did you want to have so many children?"

"I wanted — still want — more. Unfortunately Simon doesn't."

"Maybe because he wants you to himself."

"He once said he wished I'd have an affair."

Ann was shocked. "Why did he say that?"

Mabel shrugged. "Maybe he thought it would make me more

interesting for him. Maybe he thought it would make it easier for him when he had his affairs. God knows!"

She began searching in her handbag. "I've some photos here of the kids when they were babies. Would you like to see them?"

"Oh, he's beautiful, Mabel. Is this Billy?"

"Yes, at six months. And here's Allan at three months. And this is a good one of the twins on their first birthday."

For the rest of her visit Mabel spoke of her children with a beacon of pride shining in her eyes, and before she made to leave she showed Ann a photo of all the children and Simon and herself in Africa.

"Isn't that a good one? Don't we look a happy family? Although it wasn't all moonlight and roses in Africa. I didn't feel all that safe being the only white folks among all those blacks for a start. We were stuck away in the back of beyond. Simon liked it. He thrives on change, on anything different and of course he gave up teaching for a while and just wrote until our savings ran out. I taught our own kids because there wasn't a school. I didn't mind that but I lived in dread of any of us taking ill. I didn't like the look of the local witch-doctor."

"That sounds very insecure to say the least. I bet you're glad that episode in your life is over."

"You think life with Simon could ever be secure? Remind me sometime to tell you of our brief sojourn in India."

"He looks as if he's settled down for good now."

"Christ! Don't ever say that to him."

"Why not?"

"He might jack everything in."

"His good job you mean?"

Mabel shrugged then reached for her poncho. "Time I was away. The children will be coming home from school."

"It was nice to see you. Drop in any time."

"I will. But it's your turn to come to me now. Are you doing anything on Thursday?"

"Afternoon, you mean?"

"Or morning. Whichever you like. We could meet at the corner of Botanic Gardens, do some shopping and then have a coffee or a cup of tea in the Copper Kettle."

"Yes, that would be nice."

"After the children go to school, then. About half-past nine?"

"All right."

After seeing Mabel to the door then giving her a wave from the front room window, Ann poured herself another cup of tea and sat down. She felt more perplexed than ever. Why was Mabel making such a point of cultivating a friendship with her? And why was she so anxious for her relationship with Simon to continue? Especially when she obviously knew that Simon had had love affairs with women before.

"Do I love Simon?" Ann asked herself. She wasn't sure of the answer to that either. What was love? Was it the safety and security that Charlie had so conscientiously given her for nearly thirty years? Was it the faithful and conscientious devotion she had given to Charlie for these same years? She had been devoted to Helen too but she didn't think she had allowed her anxious love for the child to interfere with her concern for all Charlie's needs, physical or emotional.

But everything had gone wrong — or so it seemed — between her and Helen. Between her and Charlie. And it had nothing to do with Simon. It had all gone wrong before she met him.

She studied Simon closely at the meeting of the next class. There were quite a few new students, all much younger people, Ann noticed. They settled themselves confidently on the front row and it became obvious that two of them, mere girls in their twenties, were determined not only to impress but to attract the tutor sexually. She detected the glimmer of enjoyment in his eyes and the subtle swagger in his movements, although he afforded the girls no more time or attention — less if anything — than the other students. No extra charm was meted out to them, yet it was obvious that the men were not nearly so enamoured with Simon as the women were. He always encouraged class participation and on this occasion, with the increased numbers present, a verbal fight for talking-time had developed.

In the middle of it, just when the discussion was at its liveliest and most intersting, the janitor banged on the door and bawled, "You're away past your time, you lot! I'm going to lock up."

Such loud groans of protest and disappointment arose that Simon smiled and said, "All right, all right. You're all welcome to come round to my place until we thrash this out."

He began packing his briefcase, completely ignoring the cheer of delight from the class, the bustle towards the door and the general chatter about who could give lifts and who needed lifts. It wasn't the first time she had noticed this ability to alternate between concentrated interest and complete withdrawal. But it always made her feel somwhat uneasy. On this occasion, thinking of Mabel, she felt panicky as well. One's husband descending unexpectedly with such a mob of people just before the evening meal was enough to give any woman a heart attack — even if she hadn't four children to attend to.

"I doubt you've had it tonight, Ann."

Startled, she turned to Jessie who was standing nearby buttoning up her coat.

"What?"

Jessie jerked her head in Simon's direction. "You usually get a lift with 'Supersex', don't you? But it looks as if these youngsters are trying to get him to take them. Come on, there's room for one more in my car."

Ann followed the other woman, glancing back before leaving the room. Her eyes met those of the tutor but she had no idea what he was thinking.

As soon as she and Jessie reached Hilton Gardens she ran ahead to warn Mabel.

"Christ!" Mabel said. "Come on in, Ann. Just leave the door open for the rest of them."

She was wearing a floral wrap-round apron and checked carpet slippers and looked very comforting and motherly.

"Fancy a cup of tea?"

"But there's all the rest of them," Ann said.

Mabel shrugged. "I've got two big teapots and a coffee pot."

"I'll help you, then. I'll put the cups out on a tray and carry them through."

"I wonder what I've got to eat?"

"They won't be expecting food, surely! They'll just wait for a half-hour or so's chat and then go."

Mabel sauntered over to a pantry cupboard and stood gazing unperturbed at the chaos inside. "If they do it'll be the first time."

"You mean this has happened before?"

"Uh-huh."

"And you've had to give them all something to eat?"

"Just a few sandwiches or something. They don't come for the beer. How about sardines? There's a half-dozen and more tins here. Why the hell did I buy so many sardines?"

"I'll open the tins," Ann said, already feeling harassed. "You get the bread out. How much bread have you got? You can't have enough bread. No, you haven't! Oh, Mabel, it's too bad of him doing this to you."

Mabel laughed. "He doesn't do it on purpose. He's just a bit thoughtless."

"He seems to me to be quite the reverse. I mean, very earnest and thoughtful."

"Yes, he's that too."

"How can he be both?"

"I dunno."

Waves of voices could be heard rising and falling in the sitting-room.

"I'll run out for a few loaves!" Ann said. "The Pakistani's will still be open."

"Don't be daft. I'll send one of the kids."

"Where are they?"

"Through with their dad, I suppose. They enjoy all the arguments. I'll go and tell Billy."

Plucking a sardine from one of the tins that Ann had just opened, Mabel tossed it into her mouth and went away chewing contentedly and wiping her fingers on her apron.

The tins were all opened, the sardines mashed up with salt and pepper and vinegar and what bread there was in the kitchen buttered and made into sandwiches and still Mabel had not returned.

Eventually a tall young lad appeared. She could see the resemblance to Simon: the same enigmatic grey eyes, the same dark hair and lean frame. Only Simon was taller with the set shoulders of a man.

"You must be Billy," Ann said. "I'm Mrs Sommerville."

"How do you do?" the boy said gravely and put out his hand. The resemblance unnerved her. "Has your mum given you the money for the bread?"

"No."

She reached for her handbag. "Here, take this fiver and get three large loaves . . . no, better make it four, and half a dozen packets of biscuits."

"My mother will give me the money."

"It's all right, Billy. Your mother will square up with me later when we've more time. You go to the Pakistani's with that just now. Please?" she added with an appealing smile.

He left without saying any more.

Ann stood gazing at the disaster area of a kitchen with its work-surfaces crammed with tins and paper bags and bottles and cutlery and dishes and women's magazines and remnants of food. Then, unable to resist the challenge of it, she rolled up her sleeves.

Chapter Twenty-Two

"WELL, THANK you very much for your kind help!" Ann said sarcastically.

Mabel laughed. "I'm sorry, Ann. I got caught up in such a fascinating discussion. I forgot all about you."

"Charming!"

"Christ! You've done all the sandwiches!"

"And washed the dishes."

"You didn't need to do that."

"There weren't any clean ones. Have you been sitting through there calmly knitting?" she asked, her voice rising incredulously when she noticed what Mabel was holding.

"And listening," Mabel said.

Ann shook her head. "I don't understand you."

"Come on through. Simon will be missing you."

"I just do not understand you," she repeated, following Mabel across the hall and into the sitting-room.

A sexy girl in tight jeans that clung to the contours of everything was squatting on the floor at Simon's feet and trying hard to appear intelligent. The others were all either sitting on chairs or on the floor and were engaged in an argument with Simon. Apparently the only person agreeing with him was the sexy girl who was called Rosemary.

Ann found a space on the floor.

"I see Simon's point." Rosemary's eyelashes fluttered and her husky voice kept repeating, "He's perfectly right, of course!"

Eventually Ann felt so irritated she could bear it no longer. "I don't agree," she burst out. "His argument, it seems to me, is unsound. And, yes, I can explain why I think your argument is unsound," she added, beating Simon to it.

From then on it was like a verbal tennis match between them. She had never experienced anything so exhilarating in her life. It was as if her brain had been splashed with sparkling ice-cool water, stimulating and clarifying every thought.

At last Simon paused. His gaze thoughtfully withdrew inwards. Then he shrugged and said, "Touché."

She had a mental orgasm and he saw it. It made a smile of amusement glimmer through the veil of distant, objective interest in his eyes. His amusement infuriated her and she flushed and looked away.

Mabel said, "How about a cup of tea?"

Ann followed her back to the kitchen and once there could barely control the tremble of anger in her voice. "Did you see the way that girl's making eyes at him and he's old enough to be her father?"

"Disgusting!" Mabel tutted and helped herself to a sandwich. "You take the cups through. I'll make the tea."

"It doesn't worry you? Ogling your husband before your very eyes?"

"It's not what some do before my eyes that worries me, duckie. It's what they do behind my back. If there aren't enough cups there are some mugs lying about somewhere."

Ann's gaze sharpened with apprehension. "There are enough cups," she said, not thinking of cups. "I counted."

Mabel sighed in mock admiration. "Such efficiency!" Then, "Poor Sally's not here this term, I see."

"Sally?"

"She was pretty dim as well as being deaf, she had to lip-read, and you know how somebody like that has to watch your face intently. She sat here one night gazing up at Simon watching every word that came out of his mouth and afterwards he remarked to me what a charming and intelligent girl she was." She laughed. "He was quite taken with her."

Back in the sitting-room, tucking into sardine sandwiches and drinking tea, Mabel chatted in apparent unconcern with Jessie to a background of the record player that someone had switched on. Ann tried to join in the conversation but her attention kept straying across to the girl in the tight trousers who now perched provocatively on the arm of Simon's chair. Eventually it became such an agony to watch them laughing and talking together that Ann had to retreat to the kitchen to reason with herself and bring some sort of order to her emotions. It was ridiculous to feel like this. She knew it was ridiculous. She took deep breaths. After all, if Mabel wasn't worried, why should she worry?

When she returned to the sitting-room she found most of the occupants were dancing to the romantic music. Then she noticed Simon. He was moving slowly about the room, his hands on Rosemary's waist. She was gazing dreamily up at him, arms knotted around his neck, her body clinging close. He was smiling down at her.

A panic of distress scattered Ann's wits. Standing helplessly in everyone's way she allowed herself to be jostled about. Vaguely she perceived Mabel coming towards her.

"It's all right, duckie," Mabel said, reaching her and putting an arm round her shoulder and guiding her from the room.

In the hall Ann said shakily, "I don't feel very well, Mabel. I want to go home."

"I'll tell Simon."

"No, please!"

"Shall I phone Charlie and ask him to come and collect you then?"

"No . . . the walk . . . a breath of air . . . being on my own for a few minutes. . . . Where did I put my coat?"

"Somewhere under this pile in the bedroom, I suppose. What colour was it?"

"A belted camelhair."

"Here it is. Are you sure you'll be OK?"

"For all the distance. . . ."

"You must be more energetic than me. For me, that's one hell of a long walk."

They reached the front door.

"I'll phone you," Ann said.

She welcomed the cold air and the anonymity of the night. Turning up her collar, she walked briskly.

I must not cry, she kept telling herself. *I must act my age and be sensible.*

But she was still distraught when she reached home and had to ring the doorbell because she couldn't find her key.

She expected Charlie to meet her with a string of complaints and abuse for not being at home to serve his dinner. Instead he followed her back along the lobby. Then he went into the sitting-room. She took off her coat, put it on a hanger and hung it in the wardrobe. He was staring at the television when she went through but she could tell that his mind wasn't on it. His expression was tense and uncertain, almost furtive. She flopped down beside him on the settee and leaned back her head. And she didn't know what to say.

Her whole life, even the person she had always known as herself, had become swallowed up in a strange melting-pot and she couldn't be sure who she was any more.

"Are you all right?" Charlie said.

"I suppose so." A lump in her throat made her feel and sound like a tremulous child. "I'm just a bit tired."

"It's time you chucked that class. It's too much for you at your age."

"I'm not that old."

"Old enough to have more sense. You're just making a fool of yourself."

Tears spilled over and she got up from the settee, ashamed of her weakness but unable to do anything about it.

"I think I'll go to bed. Goodnight, Charlie."

He followed shortly afterwards and lay in the dark as quiet and still as herself. But she knew that he too was awake.

When sleep eventually overcame her it brought a wild confusion of dreams that she awoke from with an ache of unfulfilled longing.

Charlie brought her not only a cup of tea, but fruit juice and toast and honey and all on a tray.

Scrambling to a sitting position she cried out, "Oh, Charlie, you shouldn't have! You've your work to go to. I've plenty of time to get up and see to my own breakfast."

"Just eat it and shut up." He went away to get washed and shaved, hitching at his sagging trousers.

She tried to feel grateful. She tried to tell herself how lucky she was having Charlie. But nothing worked. Nothing blotted Simon from her mind. She kept thinking of their trip to Edinburgh and a few stolen hours they'd have together. But then what? She was

103

getting out of her depth and she realized it would be better to nip her relationship with Simon in the bud now before she or anyone else got hurt. Yet when the time came for the journey to Edinburgh she was ready far too early and waiting, as rosy-faced and as excited as a child for Simon to pick her up.

In the car he seemed cool and relaxed although driving so fast she found herself stiffening with tension. They didn't talk much, skirting anything personal in favour of general remarks about books or the class or what could be seen of the countryside flashing past.

She was glad to reach Edinburgh so that he would be forced to reduce speed although even in the centre of the city traffic the car still felt like a bird flying smoothly along. After finding a parking place he booked in to his hotel then took her up in the lift to his bedroom.

As he deposited his briefcase on a chair beside the bed she asked in sudden curiosity, "Don't you feel you're betraying Mabel? I do. Not to mention Charlie."

"No, I don't feel betrayal. What I give to Mabel I will still give to Mabel. In our relationship, what I give to you will be no deprivation to her. We've many sides. And maybe we need many kinds of people and many kinds of relationships to fulfil us. In many ways marriage is restrictive and unreal."

He had withdrawn behind one of his imperious looks glancing sideways and down at her.

"You're probably right," she said.

"I suggest we go downstairs for coffee and then have a look around the bookshops before lunch?"

Dutifully she followed him towards the door but before reaching it blurted out, "I love you, Simon."

The distance melted with his smile, his eyes narrowed and glimmered making her long for his touch. But he didn't touch her. Instead he opened the door and indicated she should precede him outside.

Chapter Twenty-Three

IT WAS AS if he had all the time in the world to browse around the bookshops. So engrossed was he she felt sure he'd completely forgotten her existence. He eventually chose half a dozen titles, took them to the cash desk and charmed the assistant into accepting his cheque without a bank card. He had left all his credit cards in his briefcase back in the hotel room. As they left the shop he happened to glance round at her and his face lit up with pleasurable surprise.

"You'd forgotten all about me," she accused, more incredulous

104

than angry. "If this is how you feel when I'm with you I can't imagine you ever giving me a thought when we're apart."

"Dearest Ann," he said gently. "When we're not together I miss you. Apart from your sexual attraction, you're a nice person and I so need to talk to you because of this. You set my friendly and kindly and indulgent and loving and humorous and just ordinary human feelings going again. When one doesn't use them much they get rusty. And one begins to feel a stranger to them. And a stranger to oneself."

She knew what he meant. With Charlie her ability to think, feel and live to capacity had been stultified. Only since knowing Simon was she beginning to find herself.

"If only," she said, "we'd met long ago. When we were young and free. Then we could have fallen in love and there would have been no problems. No hiding. No subterfuge. No telling lies to other people or to ourselves."

"There are always problems."

She sighed, "Yes, I suppose so."

"But they need not make us shrink from living our lives to the full. The secret is to be positive instead of negative in one's approach. Not, of course, that I am always able to do this. I get depressed. God, how I get depressed. But I do try." He stopped and gazed down at her. "What do I feel about you? You're the sun in my winter."

Princes Street bustled with lunchtime crowds and the castle towered above it in all its grey grandeur. They lunched in a tiny cellar of a restaurant with ancient bench-type seats and tables and faded brown theatre bills stuck to the walls.

She could hardly eat for excitement and was embarrassed when he noticed.

"Aren't you hungry?"

"Not very."

He selected a piece of cheese from his plate. "Let me tempt you."

He lifted it to her mouth and tucked it between her lips with provocative fingers. She almost succumbed to the desire to kiss them and trembled with the relief from embarrassment when she didn't.

They drank wine and, anxious to please him, she toasted the ultimate success of his book.

"It has a long way to go yet," he said. "As you know, what you saw was only a first draft."

"It will succeed. One day I'm sure you'll be as distinguished a novelist as you are at present a poet. You have so much talent, Simon."

His fingertips lightly explored the back of her hand. They felt like threads tingling across nerves. She was in an agony of suspense and pleasurable fear. Only with a ragged effort did she manage to retain some measure of self-control.

At last he glanced at his watch and said, "We'd better make our way back to the hotel."

They strolled along as if they'd all day instead of only two or three hours. A cold wind was blustering around them and Simon shivered with distaste.

"I hate this climate. Sometimes I think I'll go back to South Africa. It's a good country to live in."

"Only if you're a white man."

"Why do you say that? You have never been there."

"I've read all about apartheid in the newspapers and seen programmes about it on television."

"The newspapers and the media completely distort what happens in South Africa. I'm against apartheid, of course, but life isn't as bad there as people in the UK are led to believe."

She stared up at him. It occurred to her that he could have a facility of seeing events and making judgements that were convenient to his own needs. She saw it as a weakness and it saddened her.

"I may not have lived in South Africa, Simon, but I understand what apartheid means. Whites have a good life out there at the expense of the blacks. Mabel told me about all the servants you employed, for instance, and you could only enjoy their services because they were cheap labour. In that way alone you were not only condoning the system but using it to your advantage."

His attention drifted away from her towards a shop window displaying expensive men's suits.

"I taught in a black university. I was making a contribution to black culture. Servants were of no interest to me. That was Mabel's province."

They had reached the hotel and Ann's feet faltered in panic. She experienced excitement at the physical closeness of him but fear because it was the closeness of a stranger.

A gentle but firm pressure of his fingers on her elbow encouraged her inside. They did not speak in the elevator and when they entered his bedroom she glanced at her watch.

"I must catch the four o'clock train."

Regarding her with amused speculation he said, "You've time to walk back if you set off now."

She remained anxious. "You don't need to wait at the station. Just drop me off. I wouldn't want to make you late for your appointment."

106

"Relax," he said, sitting down on the edge of the bed to unpack his purchase of books and leisurely examine their titles. "Phone room service and order a drink."

She was shocked. "Then they'd know I was in your bedroom."

"Tut, tut."

Marooned, she stared helplessly at him. He laid aside the books with a smile as if he were enjoying a private joke. Then he leaned forward, caught her by the arm and pulled her on to his knee.

He kissed her tenderly and her tenseness only returned when she became aware that he was unbuttoning her blouse and loosening her bra. But his hands caressing her breasts soon submerged her again in sensual pleasure. He slid her round until she was lying on the bed. She began to moan, half-fearfully, as his hands explored under her skirt.

"Relax," he soothed. But she trembled weakly as he removed her skirt, then her panties. His fingers found the warm wetness between her legs and an ecstasy that she had never experienced before astonished her. It quickened her moans to a kind of panic as Simon entered her.

Afterwards, lying in his arms she felt dazed. He looked perfectly still and calm lying on his back, eyes closed, one arm cradling her, the other pillowing his head.

"Are you sleeping?" she asked eventually.

"No."

"What time is it?"

He brought his wrist down in front of his face and opened his eyes. "Quarter past three."

"I'd better get ready."

"Oh, yes. Now that you've had your way with me just cast me aside."

Laughing she sat up, "Don't look."

"I think you look beautiful."

Too shy to meet his eyes for more than a second, fiery-cheeked and happy, she quickly dressed then went over to comb her hair at the mirror.

"I don't want to miss my train."

He sighed and swung his legs from the bed. " I don't feel like this bloody lecture tonight. Come to think of it — I never feel like bloody lectures."

"You're a good teacher."

"I know. But I'd rather be a good writer. A full-time writer." He smoothed back his hair. "I keep telling myself I will be one day, but time is getting short. It's now I should be writing full time. Now!"

He got up and padded, naked, through to the bathroom. When

107

he re-emerged he was dressed and his hair had obviously been combed.

"Ready?" he asked.

She nodded and he gave her a brief tender kiss before opening the door. While he was driving her to the station she kept glancing round at him. She loved his dark hair, and the way he had of occasionally smoothing it back with his fingers. She loved everything about him, his gentleness, his warmth, even his enigmatic coolness, the way he could distance himself from her as, for no apparent reason, he was doing now.

As they neared the station he said, "Are you sure you don't want me to come in with you?"

"No, there's no point. You'll only make yourself late."

When they arrived he leaned across and opened the door at her side. "Safe journey."

"You too," she said getting out.

He shut the door then, without looking round at her, lifted one hand from the steering-wheel in a brief gesture of goodbye before driving away.

Later, in the train on the way home, she leaned back and, pretending to be asleep, relived over and over again the experience of the afternoon. Until her cheeks burned and she felt embarrassingly wet and had to open her eyes and try to concentrate on looking out of the window.

She longed for Simon to make love to her again. It was as if she had taken a shot of heroin and become addicted. She hoped he would be thinking about her but doubted it. She feared that she was not only a separate but a very small and relatively unimportant part of his life. It seemed to her that Simon would be able to take her or leave her. Whereas already she was totally involved and unable to contemplate life without him. She was still in his arms. She still felt him moving inside her when she reached her destination, and as she made her way to Canal Lane.

The entrance, the stairs, the flat was quiet and empty. She peeled off her coat and hung it in the wardrobe, the need for Simon becoming more and more acute. The need frightened her. She had never envisaged this tide of emotion that threatened to engulf her and knock her completely off balance. She began to feel uncertain, even suspicious like someone forced to seek protection against a devious opponent.

Preparing Charlie's dinner, she found comfort in familiar routines. Setting the table and sweeping the kitchen floor made her feel safe. Until the telephone rang and she tensed with apprehension.

"Hi, there," Mabel's voice had a studied casualness. "How's tricks?"

108

"I'm fine. How are you?"

"I 'phoned this morning but you weren't in."

"I was at the shops, I suppose."

"Aren't you sure, duckie?"

Ann forced out a laugh. "You know me."

"Uh-huh."

"I've a terrible memory."

"I popped up in the afternoon. Like you said — 'Pop in any time you're passing.'"

"Oh, I'm sorry. I'm usually in."

"That's what I thought."

Tension was screwing the muscles at the back of Ann's neck and head. She could hardly think for the pain.

"I was browsing around bookshops. You know what I'm like with books."

"Uh-huh. Oh, well."

"Come tomorrow. For coffee. Or afternoon tea. I'll bake some more of these biscuits you liked so much. And one of my chocolate cream cakes."

"There's no need to sound so guilty, duckie."

"I'll see you tomorrow, then?"

"Sure, why not? I'll have to go out for some fruit and vegies in the afternoon. I like to kids to have plenty."

"I'll look forward to seeing you then."

Mabel gave one of her odd little laughs before she hung up.

Chapter Twenty-Four

"I MISS him," Mabel said through a mouthful of cake. "I even miss him nagging at me."

Crumbs spluttered down over her bell-tent of a blouse and she calmly flicked them off. There had been cream too. It left a greasy stain on the flame-coloured satin. Mabel looked as if she couldn't care less.

"He said he'd only be away two or three days. But you can never tell with him."

"Hasn't he phoned?"

"Oh, yes, he's good at phoning."

Not to me, he's not, Ann thought bitterly.

Mabel picked her teeth for a minute. "The kids miss him too. They're very proud of him."

"He's a very clever man."

"Very."

"Good-looking too."

"You noticed!"

"Would you like another bit of cake?" Ann queried anxiously. Mabel laughed. "I know what your little game is."

"What?" Ann tried to ignore the stab of pain in her head.

"You're trying to make me fat."

"No, honestly." Relaxing with relief, Ann changed the subject. "How did the twins get on with their violin lessons? Did they go in the end?"

The last she'd heard they hadn't been too keen but apparently it was the policy of the school to encourage some sort of musical commitment. Mabel always enjoyed talking about the children and the next half-hour passed pleasantly enough.

"Christ, look at the time," she announced at last. "They'll be in and no tea ready. I'd better go."

Ann helped her on with her coat and kissed her at the door. "It was nice seeing you, Mabel. Come as often as you like."

She had never kissed Mabel before. Or fussed over her so much. Despising herself, she went through to the front window and stood smiling and waving until Mabel's small, lazily-moving figure drifted out of sight.

Then she took a couple of aspirins before clearing away the tea things and preparing Charlie's dinner.

She was nice to Charlie too and when Helen and Dave dropped in later on their way to a folk concert, Helen kidded her father about what a good mood he was in.

They had all been laughing together over something Charlie said when the 'phone rang. Thinking it might be Simon, Ann hurried in a mixture of joy and apprehension to answer it.

A strange voice surprised her by announcing that it was a neighbour of her mother's. Then the voice went on to say, "I'm sorry, Mrs Sommerville, your mother's had a stroke. They've taken her away to the hospital."

Frantically Ann dialled the hospital number, shouting at the same time, "Helen, Charlie — Grandma's ill. I'm trying to get through to the hospital."

Both Charlie and Helen came through to the lobby and stood waiting as she was put through.

"Mrs Fenton?" a voice at the other end said. "Yes, but I'm afraid I've bad news for you, Mrs Sommervile. . . ."

Helen came nearer and touched her arm but Ann ignored her.

". . . Mrs Fenton was dead on arrival."

"Oh, no."

Helen prised the receiver from her hands, linked arms with her and led her back to the sitting-room.

"Mum, she was old. It had to happen sometime."

110

The television was on. Ann stared at it, tears pouring down her face.

Helen nudged Charlie, "Dad, switch that off, for pity's sake!"

Charlie hastened to do as he was bid but he said, "Come on, come on, Annie. Letting yourself go like that won't bring your mother back. Try to control yourself for once."

The death had come as such a shock. The finality of it was too terrible to accept. The child in her had always optimistically believed that her mother would forgive her and see her and speak to her again. Somehow, sometime, her mother would be persuaded to love her as she'd always loved Constance. The woman in her knew that her mother would never love her, never even like her. The death had come as a punishment for her sins.

Charlie gave her extra housekeeping money in case she'd be short after making all the funeral arrangements, and on the night of the funeral he said kindly, "Do you want me to come into bed beside you?"

She was glad to lie cuddled close in his arms until the sleeping tablet that she'd taken blotted out the memories of her home when she was a child, and when her mother and father and Constance were alive. Sleep blocked the panic of impermanence, the black hole of nothingness into which her life was draining away and disappearing. She wanted to talk and the spectre of depression that was the skeleton in her mind, the follower in her footprints, the shadow at the corner of her eye. She longed to talk to Charlie and seek deeper comfort than touching could bring. But she had found by bitter experience that it was impossible to talk to Charlie about anything serious or even anything that interested her. If she tried, he had always been embarrassed, or bored, or crushing, or all three. In the face of her seriousness or interest or enthusiasm he had mastered the art of the sarcastic eyebrow, the wide yawn, the down-to-earth interjection like, "I fancy a sausage for supper."

On the day before the funeral Mabel had called and Charlie had answered the door.

"Annie's mother just died," she heard him say. "The funeral is tomorrow. Come on in."

"Christ! No, I won't come in, Charlie. Tell Ann . . . hell, what can anyone say? Tell her I'm sorry."

There was no communication of any kind from Simon.

Life went on, day after day, night after night. Yet at the same time she seemed to have lost touch with life. She felt cast adrift. Her father, her sister and now her mother had gone. Their blood had been her link, her place in the eternal scheme of things. They were her belonging. Now she was cut off and frighteningly alone. She needed her own flesh and blood.

111

Time and time again she gravitated towards East Doltan and Helen, only to turn back without reaching the flat. Once she had hovered at the entrance of Helen's building almost overcome with the need to be with her. Once she'd even gone up in the lift and stood at her door with hand raised ready to knock. Eventually she had left without knocking. She knew it wouldn't be fair to burden the girl with her grief. Helen had been kind and supportive before and during the funeral. But she was young and had her own life to live with Dave.

Then one day she was wandering aimlessly up Byres Road when a hand touched her arm and she turned to see Simon gazing down at her.

"I'd like to talk to you. Can you come for a cup of coffee somewhere?"

She shrugged and looked away without replying.

"There's a craft shop down this lane and round the corner," he told her. "It has a place upstairs." Cupping her elbow in his hand he guided her firmly along.

Once they were settled in the small room that served as a wholefood restaurant he said, "I was so disturbed to hear of the death of your mother. I wanted to write. I wanted to phone. I wanted to come and see you. I did none of these things. It was very remiss of me to leave it so long before contacting you." He shook his head, "But these things scare me. I feel so inadequate in the face of them. I suppose it is because, at bottom, nothing helps. At least, nothing ever has for me."

"Are your parents dead?"

"My father took ill while I was abroad. I had dreaded this for a long time. I had intended to go back to Britain and take care of him. I wanted so much to give him comfort and friendship in his last years. I had wanted to make some money from my writing in order to do this — but, while I was still abroad, he died."

"Simon, I'm sorry."

"I was inconsolable. I felt like a traitor, callous, cruel, selfish."

"No, you shouldn't have felt like that. . . ."

Avoiding her eyes he said, "I didn't intrude in your private grief, Ann. Maybe I should have? That could be just another of my mistakes. But, believe me, I felt for you, my sorrow was with you."

Their coffee arrived and after a few sips she broke the silence by asking, "Is your mother dead too?"

For a minute or two he didn't answer and when he did she detected the reluctance in his tone and the subtle distancing from her.

"She may well be. She left my father and me when I was twelve. I've never heard of her since."

"She divorced your father, you mean — and he was awarded custody of. . . ."

"No, one evening she just walked out of the house. She and my father had been quarrelling. I was in bed but I was awake and I heard them. Then the outside door banged. And that was it."

"She never even said goodbye to you? How could any mother be so cruel to her own child? How must you have felt? To be rejected like that!"

He gave her one of his cool patronizing looks. "I was brought up by a doting aunt and enjoyed a particularly happy childhood."

Still, she couldn't help wondering if such a traumatic experience had affected his character. And if so, in what way? Could it have inflicted the same kind of erosion to self-esteem as her mother's rejection of her?

Coloured by her grief and memories of her own childhood, the question harrowed her. Until he took her hand in his.

"Do you want to talk about your mother, Ann? Perhaps that will help." He waited in the silence that followed.

"She would have nothing to do with me."

Crease lines formed on his brow but he did not speak.

"She blamed me for my sister's death. It was proved it wasn't my fault. Yet sometimes I have such terrible nightmares. I've never driven a car since."

"What happened exactly?"

She told him.

"Obviously it wasn't your fault, Ann."

She wasn't hearing him or seeing him although her eyes still rested on his face. "If only she had forgiven me."

"Why do you feel guilty?"

She did not answer.

"Ann," he insisted. "Think about it. You have no logical reason to feel remorse. Grief, yes. But not guilt or remorse."

After a minute or two he repeated, "Think about it."

"I have thought about it. My mind tells me there's no logical reason to feel guilty. I *know* I wasn't responsible for my sister's death. I *know* my mother was wrong to make me suffer like that. Yet I still *feel* guilty, Simon. I feel guilt in the very marrow of my bones. I don't think it will ever go away. It's part of me."

"It sounds as if a pattern of guilt had been formed long before the accident."

For a time she was silent again.

"Yes, that could be true."

"It might help to read Bertrand Russell's book *The Conquest of Happiness*. In it he says that whenever you begin to feel remorse for an act which your reason tells you is not wicked, you should —

among other things — examine the causes of your feeling of remorse and convince yourself in detail of their absurdity."

She smiled wanly at him as he went on in his precise, school-masterly way. "His theory — or one of his theories — is that you should let your conscious beliefs be so vivid and emphatic that they make an eventual impression on your unconscious strong enough to cope with the impressions made by your mother when you were an infant."

"No doubt he's right in theory."

"Why don't you get the book? Study it. Try putting his theories into practice. Try examining your irrationality closely. Be determined not to respect it and not to let it dominate you. If it thrusts foolish thoughts or feelings into your consciousness pull them up by the roots, examine them, reject them."

She nodded but tears began spilling down her face. "I know this sounds crazy," she said, "but recently I've been thinking of my first boyfriend. He died." She shook her head unable to go on.

"No, I don't think you're crazy. Maybe this is your grieving time for him too. Come on." He put an arm round her and helped her up. "I'll take you back down to the car."

And there, in his arms, yet hardly aware of him, she wept until she was exhausted.

Chapter Twenty-Five

YOUNG PEOPLE it seemed, just did what came naturally and that was that. It had been different in her day. She had been brought up with one strict set of rules, the Ten Commandments.

They had hung in crimson and royal blue and gold letters framed on her bedroom wall at her mother's house. All the picture books she'd ever had as a child had been of a biblical nature with pictures of Jesus and lambs. For her twenty-first birthday she had been given a present of a new Bible. THOU SHALT NOT COMMIT ADULTERY was one of the rules she had always accepted as law. Now she was haunted by the secret terror that somehow her mother knew she had broken this law and despised her for it. She daren't think of Constance either without mounting shame and fear. She vowed to harden herself against Simon. But he only needed to glance at her and all her stern resolutions immediately melted away.

They had never actually made love again since the first time in Edinburgh. There had never been an opportunity. Until, when Simon was seeing her home on one occasion, he stopped the car in the lane and said, "I'm going to be alone in the flat for a couple of days. If I give you a key will you be there when I return from the university tomorrow?"

"Where will Mabel and the children be?"

"They are going to a family gathering in Newcastle. The whole clan will be there, including her mother. It's an elderly relative's golden wedding celebration, I believe."

He slid the key into her pocket, his fingers sending waves of ecstacy from her hip into her groin.

"I'll be home at three o'clock" he said.

For the rest of the evening with Charlie she alternated between furtive-eyed evasiveness and bursts of desperate affection. Next day she tried to cover up by being extra attentive to him. She called him darling and grilled a nice bit of steak and onion for his rolls at lunch. He rewarded her with a big kiss and a bear-hug that made her feel worse. After he'd gone the crazy jigging of her pulse began to frighten her. It was impossible to relax as she bathed and changed into new underwear she'd bought. Black lacy bra and suspender belt and black nylon stockings. She studied her reflection in the mirror. She was slimmer than many women of her age. The sexy underwear revealed no repulsive spare tyres. Her skin was good except for a few stretch marks caused by pregnancy. But she was a middle-aged woman and the glow and resilience of youth had long since faded from her flesh. She was no dolly-bird either. Turning away from the mirror she wriggled into a neat fawn shirt-waister dress, zipped up her boots, belted on her coat and left the house.

Approaching Simon's flat it occurred to her that probably the neighbours knew that Mabel was away and they would see her go in. One of them might even tell Mabel.

For a minute or two after shutting the door she leaned against it, staring at the deserted ballroom of a hall. Eventually she crossed over to the kitchen. Mabel's floral apron was draped on the back of a chair. She could not have felt worse had she been confronted with Mabel herself. Retreatingly hastily from the kitchen she found the sitting-room. It was as if she were a criminal, a desecrator of someone else's home. Worse, she was here to betray a friend. Distracted, she went over to the window to watch for Simon, then retreated again for fear of being seen.

If only he had been here to welcome and reassure her it might have been different. But despite the fact that she had purposely arrived ten minutes late he had not been waiting. The slow passing of time marked her agony. She kept telling herself to relax, not to be stupid. After all, it wasn't as if she was going to commit murder, or even to break up a marriage. She never had and never would have any intention of breaking up Mabel's marriage.

115

After half an hour in the sitting-room she began pacing through the house. Every room told a story of lives in which she had no part. Children's socks and school books lay around. A teddy bear sat straight-backed and stiff-armed against a pillow. Washing dangled from a bathroom pulley. A book lay open on the breakfast table. A double bed had rumpled sheets and dented pillows.

He still hadn't come after an hour.

Sick with humiliation, she decided to leave. And yet — what if he'd had an accident and the police or the hospital telephoned? Eventually her head began to throb with anger. Hadn't he done this before? Kept her waiting and waiting until she felt ill. What was his idea? What did he expect to gain by such behaviour?

Of course, time appeared to mean nothing to his friends either. Zoë, she'd learned, often kept a man waiting for hours because on the way to his flat she had got involved (and drinking) with someone else. It seemed that all was confusion and disorder with the lot of them. Except in the area of their work. Perhaps it was because the academic, the intellecual side of their lives was so concentrated, so conscientiously objective that the other areas disintegrated into selfishness, neglect and confusion.

She didn't know. She didn't want to know. They were too much for her. She couldn't cope with them. Her anger frittered away. Depression replaced it, weighing down on her so heavily it suffocated every other emotion. It oozed through every vein. It clogged and fuddled her mind. It blurred her vision. It distorted her hearing and distanced her from her surroundings. Slumped in a chair in Mabel's sitting-room, sounds of the clock inside and the traffic outside became muffled echoes from another world.

She did not hear Simon enter the house. When she saw him she rose but still disorientated with depression and unable to relate to him.

"Hello, Ann," he murmured in his elegant, polished voice. "How are you? I'm sorry I'm late. My students were very keen today. We became involved in a very. . . ."

Unexpectedly she heard herself say, "You bastard!"

She began to tremble. A confusion of emotion rushed in to fill the void. She needed him to take her in his arms to comfort her and soothe away the anguish. But at the same time she hated him for being the cause of it.

"Who do you think I am? Your down-trodden, adoring *hausfrau* of a wife? Well, maybe you can treat her like this but not me. It never even occurred to you to 'phone. You bastard!"

He raised an eyebrow. "Quite a virago. I'm surprised."

"Oh, are you? Are you indeed? Well, here's another surprise." She flung the key at him. "You can stuff that!"

116

Flying from the room she suddenly had the sensation of careering towards the terrifying void of her life, being sucked through space towards black nothingness. She stopped at the outside door, clinging to it for a few minutes, anchoring herself. Eventually she returned to the sitting-room.

"I'm sorry," she said.

He had a closed face but he opened his arms to her. Relaxing helplessly against his body she added, "But you are a bastard. Over an hour I've been sitting here worrying."

"You know what the students are like. It can be very difficult to get away. I thought you would understand."

"I don't believe you thought of me at all, Simon."

"Oh, well. . . ." He shrugged and made to turn away but she clung to him.

"Don't let's quarrel."

"I am not quarrelling."

"Please love me."

He sighed and gathered her close to him, "Darling, I do love you, I do."

His lips caressed her ears and neck then hardened with sudden passion over her mouth. He undressed her quickly and pulled her down on to the rug in front of the fire. He cupped her breasts tightly together and squeezed his rigid penis between them. In an ecstatic frenzy he took his pleasure of her. Never before even in dreams had she experienced love-making such as this. It excited her, caught her by the throat so that she could hardly breathe. But at the same time she was afraid of his passion.

Afterwards they lay quietly in each other's arms. Then he smiled down at her. "I can still feel your heart racing."

"It's time I was racing." She sat up and reached for her clothes.

He tried to detain her by gently sliding his fingers into the moist folds between her legs.

"Simon, look at the time," she protested.

"Love me," he said. "Not passively, not just allowing me to make love to you."

Unsure of what he was meaning she regarded him with some anxiety.

"I adore you making love to me."

"I know, darling. But don't you want to make love to me?"

"Simon, I really will have to go. I must be home before Charlie. Sometimes I think he suspects what's going on. He's been acting very strangely."

After a moment or two Simon began pulling on his own clothes. "I'll drive you home."

"No I'd rather you didn't. He might see us."

117

It was true what she'd said to Simon about Charlie. Returning to Canal Lane she thought about the strained silence between them, the long awkward spells that were quite different from their previous lack of conversation. At best, only half Charlie's concentration was on television or his newspaper these days. And as often as not when she attempted to speak to him it was like treading on a minefield.

The most innocent of questions could make Charlie explode with glee and derision. "What? You don't know who was the President of America in 1944? You who thinks you're so clever?"

On the slightest provocation, or completely out of the blue, he would try to gain points over her by quizzing her on general knowledge.

"What's the capital of Turkey?" he'd suddenly burst out. Or, "Where was the Armistice signed after the first World War?"

Sometimes he'd sneer, "You're not that clever!"

"I never said I was clever," she'd indignantly protest.

"You've never been out of the country. I've crossed the desert with a gun. I've fought my way across Italy. . . ."

"I'm not disputing the fact."

"Yes . . . well . . . you'd better not try."

That night, as usual, Charlie made straight for the bathroom. When he emerged again he announced, "It's Randolph Scott tonight." He seemed perfectly normal and she was grateful. But to be on the safe side she kept a nervous distance from Charlie, busying herself with stirring the soup then dishing it and bustling with it through to the table in the sitting-room. She was afraid Charlie would be able to see her sexual experiance of the afternoon as if she were a television screen. Or smell it from her. Although as soon as she'd returned to the house she'd washed between her legs and sprayed herself with deodorant.

They supped their soup, automatically their eyes on the newscaster. Afterwards they watched "Coronation Street". Then there was a variety show compered by a particularly infantile comedian who pulled funny faces and wore baggy trousers. Then came the Western. Listening to the familiar drawl, watching the usual plot move to its inevitable conclusion, she hung in space, nervous spasms building up in her head.

At the usual time, during one of the commercial breaks Charlie rose, and stretched, and scratched his belly and said, "Time for supper. What do you fancy? A jam doughnut or a cream sponge? I fancy a jam doughnut myself."

"You and your fucking jam doughnuts!"

Charlie was so horror-struck he collapsed back on to the settee.

"That's terrible! You've never heard filthy language like that

118

from me."

She felt shocked herself. She didn't know why she'd said it.

"I'm sorry, Charlie."

"So you should be." Charlie was red in the face with indignation. "It's enough to make your mother turn in her grave."

She immediately collapsed inside like a little girl. She wanted to speak to her mother. She wanted to tell her she was sorry. Just once again.

Chapter Twenty-Six

"REMEMBER UNCLE Bert?" said Charlie, looking up from the letter that had come for him in the morning post.

Ann shook her head.

"Of course you do, stupid!" Charlie insisted. "He's my mother's brother. Or was. He's dead. Died yesterday. The funeral's on Wednesday."

"He was the one in Aberdeen," Ann said, remembering.

"We'll have to go up there for the funeral. I'll have to ask a couple of days off my work this afternoon."

The thought of spending two or three days with Charlie's relations appalled her. "Oh, Charlie, must I go?"

"You're my wife!"

"Yes. Not your Siamese twin. There's no reason why you shouldn't go by yourself. You know how funerals upset me."

"Don't be daft. He's not your uncle. Why should you be upset?"

"It's just funerals. They make me so sad remembering my father and mother and Constance. No, I won't go, Charlie. I'm sorry."

"But what'll Aunty Jessy think? Your place is with me. It's a disgrace."

"Oh, Charlie."

"Never mind the 'Oh, Charlie'. If you won't go, I won't go."

Claustrophobia snapped at her heels. "I can't bear this."

"Can't bear what?"

"I don't even want to talk to you. You're impossible."

Charlie looked affronted. "All I did was ask you to go to my Uncle Bert's funeral."

"You go."

"But how would you manage here on your own? You've never been on your own before and you know how stupid and nervous you are."

"I'll be all right, Charlie. Believe me. Now you'd better get away to your work or you'll be late."

More and more she was experiencing a sense of being released from a strait-jacket every time Charlie left the house. The thought

119

of his being away for two full days and nights was absolute bliss.

She told Simon about it when he phoned that afternoon and he said, "Would you really enjoy being on your own? Or would you like to come with me to Paris?"

She thought she had not heard him properly. Or that he had been joking. Cautiously she echoed, "Paris?"

"I've been invited to give a paper at a conference at the Sorbonne at the end of the week. I could phone and have them bring the date forward." After a minute he added, "Ann, are you still there?"

"Yes."

"Will you come?"

"This may sound foolish, Simon —" she made an attempt at a laugh — "A woman of my age! But I've never been abroad before. Nor have I ever been in a plane."

"Ann!" His voice was gentle but she imagined it held a note of reproof.

"Charlie always just likes to go to Millport." She closed her eyes, ashamed of how feeble she sounded.

"Will you come?" he repeated.

Her heart palpitated at the enormity, the impossibility of it all.

"I haven't got a passport."

"Go to the post office and get one of those temporary things. I'll book your flight with mine."

"I'd need to go to the bank."

"Well?"

"All right."

"Do it now. And go to the post office."

"All right."

"I'll phone you back later about the flight."

She was shaking from head to foot by the time she put the phone down. Just for a few seconds her thoughts retreated with longing to the safe humdrum routine of life without Simon. But excitement soon flooded back to sweep her along.

She still couldn't credit it was happening though. There was a terrible suspenseful hassle before Charlie could be persuaded to go to Aberdeen on his own. But eventually he left carrying his pyjamas, a clean white shirt and black tie and his shaving gear in her zipper shopping-bag. He looked so uncertain and self-conscious without her that her heart gave the same kind of wrench of sympathy and rapport with him that she had experienced long ago in their courting days. She waved from the window not believing that she was about to fly in an aeroplane, set foot in a foreign country and spend the night with another man.

Yet only a few hours later she was with Simon in the airport. She was wearing her Russian-style dress and boots and belted camelhair coat. He was more handsome than she'd ever seen him, in a lounge suit that looked as if it had been not only cut in Saville Row but the very fine, muted checked material had been especially woven for him. She had never seen a material like it before. It added to his distinguished appearance.

His elegance and his lean intelligent face increased her sense of unreality. Following him through what seemed to her a maze of intricate proceedings and different directions which he negotiated with charm and ease, she felt completely overwhelmed. Once she became separated from him in the crowd and spun around in panic like a child bereft. Then there was the long corridor that led directly into the plane, the breathless moment of claustrophobia as she stepped inside, the fluttering of nerves in her stomach as she fastened her seat-belt and realized that the plane was about to take off.

Eyes widening in a pale, tense face she appealed to Simon. He took her hand in his.

"We're going along the runway now. In a minute you'll hear the noise of the engines louden, then we're up and away as smooth as a bird until we reach Paris. You'll love it. You'll love the excitement of the flight but you'll love Paris even more."

She smiled gratefully at him and held tightly on to his hand as noise roared around her.

"You can come with me to the Sorbonne," Simon went on. "Then we'll stroll down the Boul Mich."

"The Boul Mich?"

"The Boulevard Saint Michel. We'll drink coffee in the Café de Cluny and we'll sample their delicious ice-cream. We'll sit at one of the tables outside on the pavement and watch Paris life go by."

Her eyes clung to him. "It sounds lovely."

"They I expect you'll want to see Notre Dame."

"I saw the film *The Hunchback of Notre Dame* years ago. I still remember it."

He smiled, "Charles Laughton?"

"Yes. He was marvellous, wasn't he?"

"Swinging on the bells."

"Yes! That's the scene I remember."

He patted her hand. "You can relax now. Look out of the window and enjoy the view."

Cautiously she allowed her eyes to swivel round. Then astonishment made her gape. She was held high, high in the air. Far below a beautiful patchwork of different shades of green, rust and yellow was spread out. A sense of freedom, an exquisite release flooded over her. She was floating free as a bird. It was the most incredible experience she'd ever had in her life.

"Ann."

She turned to him in a daze. "Yes?"

"What would you like to drink? The stewardess is taking orders."

"Dry Martini, please." She relaxed back, smiling at him, and he returned her smile with tenderness.

"Are you glad you came?"

"Oh, yes. Oh, thank you for bringing me."

"We must fly together again. It makes your eyes shine and your cheeks glow. You look beautiful."

The euphoria remained with her. The rather bumpy landing gave her a thrill. She found the Charles de Gaulle airport entrancing. Its teeming crowds of Africans, Japanese, Arabs, Indians, people from every part of the globe fascinated her. The men looked especially intriguing in the jewel-bright colours of their native dress. She could hardly drag her eyes away from them and their beautiful flowing robes.

Simon took a taxi to a small hotel near the Sorbonne. It was shabby and dusty and they had to climb four flights of curving stairs because there was no elevator but she didn't mind. The room had corner windows that opened out to a tiny black iron balcony and from it she could hear the continuous medley of car horns and see streets criss-crossing down below and cafés with white wrought-iron chairs and round tables decorating the pavement.

She stood on the balcony, breathing in Paris, savouring its delicious atmosphere. Behind her, at the wardrobe mirror Simon calmly straightened his tie and smoothed back his hair.

"We've time to have a coffee and a stroll around before the Sorbonne. Are you coming?"

She swirled into the room, round and round, hugging herself, unable to contain her joy. Simon laughed and caught her in his arms.

"Happy?"

"Delirious."

They walked hand in hand along the street and he pointed out interesting places to her. Then they enjoyed drinking coffee and eating ice-cream outside the Café de Cluny while they watched the busy life of Paris hurry past.

It seemed a different world from Canal Lane and Charlie.

Chapter Twenty-Seven

THE SORBONNE was an imposing building with an inner courtyard in which statues of Victor Hugo and Louis Pasteur sat in thoughtful pose. Ann and Simon went along a corridor to a large chamber with curved rows of seats and a balcony going all the way round three of the walls. Simon was met by two men who spoke to him in French. He replied — and even introduced her — in the same language. The subsequent conversation made her feel awkward, not understanding a word of it she could only smile and try to look intelligent. She was relieved when Simon indicated that she should go and sit in the audience.

Despite his conversation with the two men it still came as a surprise when Simon gave his paper in French. He seemed more of a stranger than ever as she watched and listened to him. He was someone who knew and was at ease in so many different worlds from any she had ever known. The strangeness frightened her. She needed him. She ached for him. She closed her eyes against the strange place full of strangers and willed herself to be alone with him, held safely in his arms.

After his paper there were innumerable questions, every one unintelligible to her. The bench on which she sat became harder. Time dragged. Alienation intensified.

At long last Simon and the other men on the platform — talking to each other now — came down and strolled towards one of the exits. The audience, also conversing, streamed towards doors. Ann rose uncertainly. Simon was laughing at something one of his companions had said.

It seemed to her that he had completely dismissed her from his mind. She couldn't imagine Charlie treating her like this. Charlie, in the first place, would have hauled her up beside him on the platform. When leaving he would have pounced on her and kept a grip of her, pinioning her possessively to his side.

She could hardly believe her eyes as she watched Simon saunter out of the hall apparently engrossed in an enjoyable conversation with his companions. Tears fountained up inside her chest but anger suppressed them. Pushing a path towards him, heels clicking sharply on the wooden floor she reached the corridor. There, his eyes strayed in her direction, and ingenuous surprise and pleasure immediately illuminated his face. Her anger faltered in confusion at the unexpected warmth of his expression. He was a mystery to her. She was helpless in perplexity. Then, as if to confuse her further, he said something to her in French.

"I can't speak French," she said, feeling ashamed, almost tearful, and vowing to herself that she'd start French lessons the moment she got back to Britain.

"Professor Tavarnier has invited us back to his flat."

Obviously the invitation had been extended to some of the others because seven or eight people crowded into the top floor flat and were served wine by the gaunt young professor and his tiny grasshopper of a wife.

At first there was an attempt to speak English for Ann's benefit but as the wine flowed the conversation quickened into French. Simon occasionally threw her crumbs of English translation but not enough for her to enjoy herself as he was obviously doing. She suspected that even if she had been able to speak the language she would still have had difficulty in taking part in the conversation. They were talking about people she had not met, places she had not been to and academic disciplines of which she had no knowledge.

Her anger returned. It was all so different from what she had expected. Outside of the Sorbonne she had taken it for granted that she'd spend every moment alone with Simon. It was such a chance to be on their own, an opportunity that might never come their way again. It seemed incredible that he was frittering away such precious hours. Far from making any attempt to be alone with her, Simon at one point was totally engrossed with a woman poet who was gesticulating and talking rapid, passionate French to him.

Madame Tavarnier produced food and another hour passed. And another. By the time they were strolling back to their hotel through the dark rain-shimmering streets, Ann was nearly weeping with bitter disappointment. Now he was talking about the passionate dard-eyed poet.

"She has a very impressive talent."

"Oh, I can see what she's got, all right!"

He looked round at her curiously. "Is there something wrong?"

"Something wrong? Of course there's something bloody wrong."

They had reached the hotel bedroom and she jerked and tore at the buttons of her coat then tossed it on to the bed.

"Oh?"

"You're incredible. Do you know that? You drag me all this way and then you completely ignore me."

His voice cooled. "In the first place I did not drag you here. It was your decision. You came of your own free will. Secondly. . . ."

"Don't you do your school teacher act to me. You're not in your classroom now."

He raised an eyebrow. "I fail to see the reason for this tirade but perhaps if you would try to calm yourself we could discuss the matter in a civilized way. We might even get to the root of the problem."

She didn't want a civilized discussion. She didn't feel civilized. Emotion raged inside her and she wanted to attack him, fight him tooth and claw.

"You drag me here," she shouted, "and then ignore me. You spoke to your precious friends the whole bloody night and in

124

bloody French as well!"

"You were talking with them too. I thought you would find their company and their talk interesting and stimulating. Some of the best brains and finest talent in the country were in that room."

"They were talking in French."

He shrugged. "What was to stop you reminding — insisting, if necessary — that whoever happened to be talking to you spoke English?"

"You took me there. It was your job to look after me." She felt foolish even as she said the words and her anger and frustration increased dangerously near to tears.

"Look after you?" he echoed in mild surprise. "I thought you were a capable, mature and intelligent woman."

"Damn you! You know what I mean. I thought it was going to be just the two of us. I came to Paris to be with you, not them. It's you I want to talk to not anyone else."

"Don't you think that attitude indicates the same kind of possessiveness that you object to and find so stifling in your husband?"

The idea stunned her, but she hastily rallied to her own defence. "No, I don't. At home I'm not jealous of Mabel for instance. I'm not possessive with you at the extra-mural class. This is different."

"Why?"

"The whole concept is so romantic, can't you see? Running away to Paris together."

He gave a small smile. "I hardly think accompanying me to Paris where I had to give a paper at the Sorbonne can be regarded as a romantic elopement."

"Don't you patronize me. You know what I mean."

"Never take for granted that someone else knows what you mean, Ann. Always be specific. Find the right words. Express your thoughts exactly."

"It's all thoughts with you," she said bitterly. "It's feelings with me."

"You certainly seem very distressed this evening. I'm surprised."

"I don't believe this," she said. "When a man takes a woman he loves to Paris surely it's because first and foremost he wants to be alone with her and make love to her?"

"I want to make love to you certainly."

"But not to be alone with me?"

"I'm alone with you now."

"But we've wasted the whole afternoon and evening."

"Wasted?"

"Obviously you don't see it that way."

"No."

"How can you love me, Simon? I don't understand. I've been so miserable these past few hours."

"You had no need to be. No one was forcing you to stay at the Taverniers'."

He was forcing her to examine new lines of thought and she cried out rebelliously.

"I know what you're trying to do. You're trying to shift the responsibility on to me. But the truth is you chose the form the evening would take with no reference to me and you enjoyed it without caring about me. And that's my point. Now, because you're clever you think you can twist things around to suit yourself."

He sighed. "I seem to provoke the need in you to oppose, test and counter so much of what is basic to my outlook. You feel you want to measure your mind against mine."

He was undressing and had already hung his jacket away in the wardrobe, undone his tie and neatly rolled it up and placed it on the chair over which he now draped his shirt.

She gazed at his back with its taut muscles as he bent over to remove his trousers. There was something about the way his hair peaked down at the nape of his neck and flopped forward over his brow that made her crumple inside with tenderness.

"Is that bad?" she asked uncertainly.

He went over to the bed, slid between the sheets and smoothed them over his lap.

"It needn't be. But you also want to probe and analyse me. These things can cause tension."

Conscious of his grey eyes studying her, she undressed and climbed into bed beside him. Somehow she knew that if they were going to make love — and she couldn't bear it if they didn't make love — she would have to take the initiative.

"Simon. . . ." She slid her arm over his chest. "Darling, I love you."

Shyly, curiously her hand moved down his body exploring him. The only other time in her life she'd touched a man's penis was when Charlie was making love to her and she prodded his at its root in efforts to restrain it from hurting her too much.

Now it felt good. As Simon took her into his arms she gave herself up to the enjoyment of gently squeezing and massaging him, feeling him grow and harden under her touch, feeling her desire mount with his, thrilling to the new sensation of guiding him deep inside her.

Their cries of ecstasy blended as they writhed against each other. Soon he rolled on to his back and pulled her on top of him.

"Sit up, darling. Mount me. That's right," he urged.

She sat astride him, his penis still deep inside her, his eyes

126

devouring every part of her. She felt elated. Completely liberated in mind and spirit. Then her whole body went into a spasm of passion that left her exhausted.

She rolled on to her back and closed her eyes. Then after a minute or two, Simon switched off the light.

Chapter Twenty-Eight

MABEL WOULDN'T take no for an answer. "Why can't you come to lunch? What's wrong?"

"Nothing's wrong," Ann hastily assured her.

"Well, then?"

She'd agreed eventually but cursed herself after she'd hung up the phone. Unable to settle in the house she left a note for Charlie and his lunch ready on the table and went out to do some shopping. First, though, she went into the Copper Kettle for a cup of coffee.

"Hey, Ann!"

Zoë was sitting at a corner table and waving at her to come over. Ann sat down beside her.

"Are you playing hookey?"

"No, there's no lectures this morning and my flat's as quiet as a morgue. It was beginning to depress me so I just said, 'Shit', and came out for a change of scenery. Well, how's life, Ann? Have you slept with Simon yet?"

The young waitress who was standing waiting for her order grinned down at Ann's shocked expression. Quickly recovering, Ann said, "Another cup of coffee, please."

"You looked distressed," said Zoë. "Are you in love with him?"

"I suppose I must be."

"Isn't it a load of shit?"

"How do you mean?"

"If you're in love, you suffer. At least I always do."

"I don't know about that. The worst thing as far as I can see is that it doesn't last. It seems impossible when I think of it now but I was once in love with Charlie. I mean really in love! I thought he was so big and strong and masterful."

"Maybe he was. Maybe he still is. Maybe it's just you that has changed."

Then after they had drained their cups: "Come on back to my place. I serve better coffee than this."

"I'd like to, Zoë, but I've promised I'll be at Mabel's for lunch."

"It's ages to lunchtime. What are you worrying about?"

"Well, I don't like being late and I've some shopping to do."

127

"You can do your shopping later on. The shops are open in the afternoon. The good old Pakistani's is still open at midnight. I don't think they ever shut. So why worry?"

Ann smiled her agreement but felt less than enthusiastic as she followed Zoë from the café and along the road to her flat. She knew from past experience at Zoë's what a hassle it was to get away again. It would be a miracle if she managed to get to Mabel's at all now.

"How about just having some of this instead?" Zoë made for the gin bottle as soon as they reached her living-room. "It'll save me making coffee." Not waiting for a reply she splashed out huge glasses of gin, and ignoring Ann's protests pushed one into her hands. "Sit down and relax, for Christ's sake."

Ann noticed the eagerness with which her friend downed her first drink then the sigh of relief once it was safely inside her and feared Zoë must have a drink problem. If previous occasions were anything to go by she would sit there until the bottle was finished.

It was terrible to watch such an attractive and intelligent woman deteriorate with each glass of gin, to rubber-boned, mumbling helplessness. The bottle, as usual, was emptying fast, and Zoë, as usual, was becoming over-generous.

"If you're unhappy with old what's his name — Charlie, is it? — leave him, for God's sake. You're welcome to live here with me. Be my guest. You'd probably have to doss down on the floor but what the hell! Be my guest. You're welcome here any time. You take the fucking bed and I'll doss down on the floor."

Beginning to flop and fumble already, she poured herself another drink. "Leave the male chauvinist pig!"

"It's very kind of you, Zoë. . . ."

"I mean it. You can come here any time. Be my guest."

"I know you do, but. . . ."

"Simon's a good teacher and he's a good lover."

Ann stared unhappily at her. "Have you slept with him?"

"Of course."

With one hand she bunched back her blonde hair. In the other, her half-full glass lurched to one side and spilled gin down on to the carpet.

Ann hurried over to right the glass. Then after a minute she managed to say, "You don't still sleep with him, do you?"

"Unfortunately — no. We had something great going for a while. Then it suddenly fizzled out. It wasn't anybody's fault. He was very nice about it. Very nice."

Zoë refilled the glass, nearly knocking over the bottle in the process.

"Let me go and make a cup of coffee," Ann said. "You promised me one, remember? No, don't get up. It's all right, I'll make it."

She escaped through to the kitchen. There, waiting for the milk to boil and trying not to accept how distressed she felt, she noticed the time. She was late for Mabel's already. Harassment adding to her misery, she allowed the milk to boil over while she was searching for the coffee. Then Zoë came staggering through from the living-room.

"Come through and have a drink, for Christ's sake."

"The coffee's nearly ready."

"I don't need coffee."

"Why do you need gin?"

"Oh, God! You're not going to preach at me, are you?"

Ann made two mugs of coffee and got them, and Zoë, back to the living-room.

Putting one of the mugs on the table beside her friend, she said, "Drink your coffee. It'll sober you up. I'll have to leave in a minute. Mabel will be waiting with my lunch."

"She won't mind."

"I'm late already."

"Why don't you phone her and say you can't come?"

"But I. . . ."

"You can have lunch here with me. Be my guest. We can have lunch together. We can talk all afternoon. Be my guest."

"Drink your coffee, Zoë."

Zoë's head hung slightly forward as if it were becoming too heavy to hold up. Through muddy pools of eyes she tried to find Ann's face.

"Don't go."

"I'm sorry," Ann said.

Chapter Twenty-Nine

ANN MADE her apologies and Mabel had just poured her a Martini when they heard the outside door open and footsteps in the hall.

"That must be Simon," Mabel said.

"You didn't tell me Simon would be here."

"Was I supposed to?"

Ann flushed. "No, of course not."

When Simon entered the room Mabel rose, patting her apron and saying, "Right, I'll go and rustle up some lunch. Behave yourselves, you two."

After her slippers scuffled away Simon bent over and kissed Ann, his hand sliding inside her blouse and bra and finding her nipples. She pushed him away just in time before the twins and

129

young Allan entered the room.

"Hi, Dad," Allan said.

Simon's eyes melted with affection, "Hi, son." He sat down and the twins pushed at each other in their efforts to clamber on to their father's knee.

"Right, folks," Mabel announced, entering with a tray. "Home-made soup. Can you manage it in here all right?"

"I'm sure," Simon said. "It would be more convenient for everyone if the table was set properly in the dining-room, Mabel. I'll carry the tray through. Go and help your mother put the cutlery out, girls. You too, Allan."

Loud groans of protest ensued but the children went to do as they were told. Mabel rolled her eyes.

"Such a stickler for the proprieties is Simon. OK, here's our Billy. You're just in time, son."

While they ate their soup there was much talk and laughter, especially between the children and their mother. Their father obviously played the role of stern disciplinarian or, at least, he was a stern disciplinarian compared with the easy-going Mabel. It was he who told the children to take their elbows off the table, to stop making a noise with their soup and to remember to say please and thank you. When he wasn't correcting the children he was trying to put Mabel right, betraying as he did so a fastidiousness that was painful to watch and listen to.

"Mabel, we do, I believe, have the correct size of meat plates. There's no need for our food to be heaped to overflowing on small tea plates. This is how you make extra work for yourself. The table-cover is stained with gravy already."

"I know, dear, but we can't all be good organizers like you. Shall I scrape yours on to a bigger one?"

He shook his head. "No, thank you — we also have a proper salad bowl and servers. Why have you chosen to heap everything into a soup bowl?" He looked tense and strained all through the meal and afterwards when he and the children left the house again and Ann and Mabel were doing the dishes, Ann felt compelled to ask, "Where did you meet Simon, Mabel?"

"I'm the proverbial girl next door, duckie."

"You mean, you've known him all your life? Since you were a child?"

"No, not quite."

The dishes dried and put away she followed Mabel silently back to the sitting-room.

Mabel laughed as she settled on her favourite chair and picked up her knitting. "You're puzzling over how a man like Simon could possibly pick a plain Jane like me."

"You and Simon seem so different. But you're no plain Jane, Mabel. You've got a really voluptuous figure. I've told you so before. I think you're mad not to make the most of it. I mean, you will insist on wearing such baggy shapeless clothes. And, you've got a good clear skin and handsome features. If you'd just get your hair cut professionally and buy some good make-up."

"Money, money, money."

"Surely you can't be that hard up."

"Parting with it makes me feel insecure."

After another silence broken only by the clicking of knitting needles Ann said, "Were you married when he was at Cambridge?"

"Christ, yes. He left school without an 'A' level. His father was a no-user. No wonder his mother buggered off. Drank like a fish and hardly ever worked. Never cared if Simon went to school or not. But years later Simon went to night school and took 'A' levels and eventually got a scholarship to Cambridge."

"Fancy working against such difficulties like that. I do admire him."

"I know you do, duckie."

For a man to have fought on his own against such odds and made the most of his potential instead of sinking into a rut was, to her, truly marvellous. It gave her a surge of optimism. It made her feel life was a wonderful challenge, really worth living, after all.

The next time she saw him at the class she expressed her admiration and despite his casual shrug she saw the satisfaction in his eyes.

"One has to be goal-orientated to survive. I have a long way to go before I reach my ultimate goal."

"You mean, to be a successful novelist?"

"In creative, not necessarily in monetary terms."

"Another D.H. Lawrence?"

"Lawrence was supremely himself. I want to be my own man."

"Are you working on your novel just now?"

"No."

"Oh, Simon, why not? You must finish it and get it published."

"I've had my thesis to complete. And teaching needs all one's concentration. The only creative work I've had published so far was written in Africa when I gave up my teaching post. But it was only a short work. I didn't have enough time for novel-writing then either. I should have concentrated on my creative writing years ago but I put the needs of a wife and young family first."

"Do you regret doing that?"

"No, I've never agreed with Shaw who said the true artist will allow his mother to go out to work while he stays at home. I've always put people before art — morally. If one wishes to achieve

131

one's ends at all costs, Shaw is right, that is the way to do it. If that price is too big to pay, you won't. In the past I've put my family obligation first. My writing ambition I pushed to the back. But now that the children are a bit older, it's different."

"In what way?"

"I'm determined to write full time, Ann. I'm resigning from the university as soon as I get my Ph.D."

"Oh, Simon!" She was shocked. "Your good job! And . . . and there's so much unemployment just now. It might not be easy to get another one."

"I'm not going out to work again."

"But you and your family have still got to live. Wht are you going to do for money?"

"I hope to make a living from my writing."

"Darling, I'm sure you will eventually but as far as I've heard, writers don't make a fortune overnight — or even enough to live on."

"I have a few pounds in the bank. When that runs out I'll sign on at the Labour Exchange. I'll collect National Assistance or whatever they call it."

She sighed. "I wish I could help you. You know if I had any money I'd give it to you."

"I know you would." A note of bitterness crept into his voice. "But it's Mabel who should help me and I know she won't."

"I can't imagine Mabel purposely trying to hinder you, Simon."

"She hinders me in a thousand ways. She always has. But not purposely, I agree."

"She seems very economical. She certainly doesn't spend much on herself."

"Oh, I don't want to criticize my wife. But it would make such a difference if she made the necessary effort to give me some positive help and co-operation when I need it. She could go out to work for instance after I resign."

Surprised, she said, "Do you really think it's right to expect Mabel to go out to work while you stay at home? Even though you are writing?"

He replied indignantly: "But I've gone out to work while she's stayed at home."

She was nonplussed and when some of the other students interrupted the conversation to speak to Simon she was quite glad to move away so that she could be alone with her thoughts.

Never before in her experience had a man's role in marriage, or the woman's been questioned. The man was the breadwinner. It was his responsibility to provide a home and to keep his wife and family. The wife looked after husband, home and family and tried to keep them happy and healthy. He gave financial security. She created the home and gave emotional security. If the wife went out to work it was to get a bit of pin-money or to help save for some extra expense like a wedding in the family. Or because she was bored.

The idea that it was a woman's *responsibility* to be the breadwinner just as much as a man's gave her something to think about. Once she thought about it for a while she decided that it was maybe fair enough in theory but the dice were loaded against the woman as far as putting the theory into practise was concerned. The fact that she was the one who bore the children was a drawback for a start. The women's magazines could say what they liked about how you felt better and looked better while you were carrying a child and how it was not only a painless but an enjoyable and delightful experience. It certainly was delightful once it was all over and the nurse placed your child in your arms. Before that it was a thousand small or large emotional and physical irritations that tried to drag you down and exhaust you. Until eventually, in her experience at least, and that of every woman she'd ever known, there was pain. And what pain! (Although admittedly she'd heard that nowadays there were marvellous anaesthetics.) Then there could be emotional disturbances after the birth — sometimes physical too. And there were all the exhausting anxieties about the baby's health and welfare.

Not that she regretted having a child. There were so many compensations, so many happy, loving times to be treasured. Indeed she pitied childless women.

Then of course, childless or not, there was always the menopause, the distressing emotional and physical symptoms of which were legion. She really couldn't see, taking all that into consideration, how there could be the equality that women's libbers talked about. There should be equal opportunities of course and equal pay for equal work. But so often women kidded themselves about that. She remembered Helen telling her how, after the Sex Discrimination Act had come into force she had been given the same pay as men employees in other departments. But the men had to continue carrying the heavy boxes of stock from upstairs because the girls either indignantly refused to do so or were physically incapable of doing so.

Helen had been furious at her for remarking that the men deserved extra pay in circumstances like that.

Mabel would find it very difficult if not impossible to get a job. Like herself, Mabel was middle-aged and not trained for anything in particular. And the chances were if she did get a job it would mean actually coping with two jobs because she couldn't imagine

133

Simon doing the washing, cooking, shopping and cleaning if he was at home. Mabel would still have to do it. But Mabel wouldn't be able to compete in the work market. Remembering her own humiliating efforts at job-hunting Ann didn't blame Mabel for choosing to stay safely at home with her family.

For the first time Ann thought, with conscious appreciation and gratitude, of the security and comfort and dependability that Charlie provided. Nothing could make her love him again. She shrank from any intimacy with him now and was becoming adept at excuses for avoiding sex. But the more she heard of Mabel's life with Simon the more she savoured with thankfulness the security and material comfort she'd enjoyed with Charlie.

Mabel and the children had once had to live in a most inadequate-sounding caravan in the middle of a field. Another time, in some God-forsaken spot abroad, they'd lived in a villa overrun with mice. There had been fabulous times too, Mabel was quick to point out. But aparently one never knew the minute when Simon would decide to do something different and move on.

Ann felt a cautiousness enter her. It was like when she was pregnant and instinctively began taking more care of herself, even when crossing the road. That same deep-grained self-preservation was what she felt now.

Chapter Thirty

"DOCTOR Edgington!" She kept repeating the words incredulously, proudly to herself. Simon had got his Ph.D., and she had attended his graduation. Afterwards lots of photographs had been taken then they'd had a few drinks with Simon's colleagues and friends. Then later she had gone home with Simon and Mabel and the children to share in a quiet family celebration.

"He didn't want a party," Mabel said. "He only wanted one friend here tonight and that was you."

"I'm flattered."

"I'm suspicious."

Simon said, "She's only teasing, Ann."

"Don't be too sure, duckie. But drink up. There's no need to look so worried. I'm not going to get violent. It's too much bother."

During the evening Simon read some of his poetry. One poem Mabel read with him. It was about love and marriage but not of the romantic kind. It was love with sweat and warts and all. Yet the honesty and perceptiveness, and the rhythm of the dialogue between the man and the woman, had both beauty and poignancy.

Halfway through reading her part, Mabel's voice, to Ann's horror, suddenly broke, and tears spilled down her face.

At the same time as fumbling for her handkerchief she patted Simon's hand and said, "I'm sorry, dear."

Guilt reared up in Ann like a spectre. Perhaps Mabel felt distressed and threatened because of her friendship with Simon after all. Did Mabel's calm, nonchalant exterior hide a sad and insecure woman who dreaded losing her husband? She tried to steady herself with the thought that Mabel's distress might simply be the overspill of emotion from Simon's graduation. If she, as his friend, had felt moved and proud to the point of tears during the ceremony, how much more intensely might his wife have felt?

Never, as long as she lived, would she forget the hallowed atmosphere of the old university, the awe-inspiring fanfare of trumpets, the majestic strains of the organ, the dignified academic procession in their velvet caps and regal-looking cloaks of purple, blue, crimson and gold. Then eventually the sight of Simon, his aloof expression and tall figure as distinguished-looking as ever as he walked across the platform for the conferment of his degree.

"It's been a very emotional day," she said to Mabel. "You must feel very proud of Simon."

Mabel dried off the last of her tears then gave one of her wry laughs. "Oh, he's a great guy."

Ann tried to laugh too. "Do you feel you know it all now, Simon?"

"Have you heard of Professor Joad?"

"Of 'Brains' Trust' fame? Yes, I remember hearing him on the radio."

"He once said that knowledge was like a bright torch in a dark, dark room. The more brightly it shone, the more it made you aware of how much darkness there was."

"Yes, anyone who believes that they haven't anything else to learn has a closed mind."

"He'll be after a professorship next," Mabel said.

"I told you I plan to concentrate on writing."

"Christ!" Mabel took a large swig of gin then added in a perfectly good-humoured tone. "That's all I need — being on the bloody National Assistance!"

She poured herself another drink while Simon put on some records.

"Did I tell you folks that our Billy has a girlfriend?"

"He's started young," Ann said.

"I told you he was taking after his dear old dad," she laughed. "There's a saying about menstruating — if you start young, you finish late and vice versa. I wonder if the same applies?"

135

Simon said, "As far as I remember I was six when I met my first girlfriend."

"Christ!"

"And she was five. I was very serious about her."

Mabel conducted the music with a graceful hand. "I like that one but turn the music down or the kids will never get to sleep."

"Let's dance," Simon said.

"I'm too pissed, duckie."

"I know. I was asking Ann."

Taking Ann's hand he pulled her up into his arms. Her anguish was acute. She was sure it must be obvious to Mabel how she felt about Simon. It was impossible to hide it when he held her like this.

"I don't know how the pair of you manage it," Mabel said.

Simon glanced round, eyebrow raised. "Manage what?"

"To keep so slim. It's high time both of you were having the middle-aged spread. I don't eat any more than you. But talking about eating — how about some supper?"

Ann said, "I'll have to be going soon."

"You can't go without your supper. Simon wouldn't be pleased. Would you, duckie?"

"Are you fit?" Simon asked as Mabel rose with careful, affected dignity.

"Have I ever in my life failed to give you or your friends a good supper?"

Simon laughed. "Frequently."

"Well, not tonight. Tonight I shall not let you down."

They danced in silence for a few minutes after Mabel left the room. They danced slowly, dreamily, until Ann realized that Simon's hand had slid down over her thighs.

She struggled away. "Simon, for God's sake. . . ."

"What's wrong?"

She shook her head. "I'm away to help Mabel with the supper."

He caught her arm, detaining her. "Dance with me. Slowly and gently like this. Just so that I can hold you in my arms."

With a sigh she melted into him and the big high-ceilinged roof disappeared. There was only Simon and herself, sweet-flowing into one another, and she thought, "Even if I never see him after this night, I'll always remember how wonderful it felt to be with him."

She had many other treasured moments, of course, although they hadn't had another opportunity for sex since Paris. But there was the meeting of their minds in the university class. The times they strolled through the park when, and because she was with him, the changing season took on a new, poetic beauty. She saw how the skeletons of trees donned the green gloves of spring. How the grass bloomed with purple and white crocuses before billowing with yellow daffodils.

Now the trees were resplendent in their summer gowns and the perfume of roses sweetened the air.

"Grub up!" shouted Mabel coming into the room. "And don't tell me you want it in the bloody dining-room at this time of night, Simon. You don't mind eating a plate of scrambled eggs on your knee, do you, Ann?"

"No, this is lovely, thanks."

"It's not fancy. I'm not a fancy cook. Are you? God! I bet you are! I'm a good plain cook. Eggs, minced beef and mashed potatoes, jelly and custard, not forgetting good old ice-cream. I make my own and the kids love it. Do you know something? They think I'm a super-cook and a super-mum. They once put my name in for a Super-Mum competition."

"Did you win it?"

"Christ, no. I'm only super to them. But that's enough for me."

"You've a very loving family, Mabel."

"I know. They dote on their dad too. How's the scrambled egg?"

"Delicious," Ann said.

"We might as well enjoy them while we may, duckie. Once my beloved husband starts to write full-time we won't be able to afford them."

"Thank you for the vote of confidence Mabel."

"Well, you take so long at it, dear. Could you not even type your stuff straight on to the typewriter and cut out all that scribbling first?"

"I must write in longhand first. That's the way I have to work."

"Then plod along at the typewriter with two fingers," she laughed. "Christ, Simon, we'll all be starving before you're done."

"I've told you before. You could help by taking a typing course and typing my work for me."

"Oh, no. I'm a bedmate, a cook, char, a mother to your kids, laundry-maid, nurse and general factotum. I draw the line at being your secretary as well."

He shrugged.

In the silence that followed Ann began to feel excited.

"Simon," she said eventually, "I've just had an idea. Do you think if I took a secretarial course . . . I've time on my hands . . . and I'd love to help. That is, if Mabel doesn't mind me helping you."

"Oh, Mabel doesn't mind," said Mabel, "as long as it's understood that you don't get paid."

"No, there's no question of payment. I'd enjoy typing Simon's manuscript."

"It's a generous thought, my dear," Simon said, "but I couldn't allow you to do it."

"Why not?"

Mabel answered for him. "He couldn't have anyone working with him in his precious writing-room. He keeps it locked you know. I often wonder what he hides in there."

"Only myself," Simon said. "Actually I was thinking of the money. . . ."

"I don't care about the money, Simon. I need something to occupy me. Honestly, I get so bored and restless at home. If I thought I was capable of learning to type efficiently. . . ."

"Of course you're capable. But what you should be doing, Ann, is enrolling at a university as a mature student and studying for a degree."

She was astounded. "Me? Take a degree?"

"Why not?"

She just stared at him.

"Think about it," he said.

"Meantime," Mabel said, "she could borrow your typewriter and type away to her heart's content in her own home."

"Yes, oh, please, Simon. One thing at a time. If I manage this successfully it would give me confidence to go out and tackle something else."

"If that's what you really want to do."

"Yes, it is."

"Very well."

That night she left with Simon's portable typewriter clutched in one hand. Charlie was waiting outside in the car. He now insisted in calling for her if she visited Simon's home in the evening. He gave loud blasts of the car horn to herald his arrival but always refused to come in.

"What's this?" He jerked his head in the direction of the typewriter as the car drove away.

"Simon's given me a loan of his typewriter so that I can learn to type. It'll mean I'll have a skill, Charlie. I'm so excited!"

"Why doesn't he just mind his own business?"

"Charlie, I enjoy learning. I need to keep my mind active. It's just the way I am."

"You don't need his typewriter. I can buy you a typewriter if that's what you've taken a fancy for. Have I ever denied you anything you've taken a fancy for before?"

"There's no need for you to go to all that expense."

"I can afford a typewriter as well as him. What do you bet I make more than him? These Uni guys get paid chickenfeed compared with us. What does he get in his pay packet, eh?"

138

"I've no idea what Simon earns."

"I'll find out, don't you worry."

"Charlie!"

"He's no big cheese."

"For goodness' sake! I asked if I could borrow his typewriter. I want to learn to type. It was all my idea."

"You'll give that typewriter back to that guy."

"Oh, all right."

They were silent as they reached Canal Lane and Charlie parked the car. But going up the stairs he suddenly said, "Remember that time when you were pregnant and took a fancy for Turkish Delight?"

"Yes, you were very kind."

"And that other time when you were ill and lost your appetite? The things I've done for you!"

Her voice began to strain at the edges. "All right, Charlie."

"You can't say I've not been good to you."

"Who's saying it?"

"I'll get you a typewriter, no bother. And it'll be bigger and better looking typewriter than that guy's. No bother. No bother at all."

She turned away, distressed by the sight of his trembling, wanting to spare him the humiliation of being seen, but no longer able to offer him any comfort.

Chapter Thirty-One

SIMON announced that Zoë had offered them the use of her flat and he had accepted.

Ann protested at first.

"We said we weren't going to hurt Mabel and Charlie." She wanted to add, "And what about Zoë?" — but didn't.

"Are we hurting them?"

"Yes, I think we are."

"I don't agree. If anything, my loving you makes me a nicer person to Mabel. And you've told me before that you are nicer now to Charlie than you were before."

"That's guilt."

Simon shrugged.

"Mabel must know how I feel about you, Simon."

"She's long enough in the tooth to know that people can't help how they feel."

"She's got enough to worry about with you giving up your job."

"I don't see that Zoë's offer makes much difference. We'll be lucky if we see each other alone at her place once a year. Zoë is notoriously undependable. And if she has opened a bottle before we arrive there will be no shifting her. Of course there is always your place. You are on your own there all day. What could be more convenient?"

She had remained firmly opposed to Simon's coming to Charlie's house. Being unfaithful to him seemed to her to be bad enough. To commit the infidelity under his own roof was impossible. It had been bad enough under Mabel's roof.

Then one day Simon phoned and said, "I have Zoë's key. We can have the place to ourselves this afternoon."

"Oh, Simon."

"You'll come?"

Love and excitement stirred in her veins, a potent brew that rapidly dispelled caution.

"When?"

"Now."

"I'm on my way."

Long before she had reached the flat she was in a fever of desire and as soon as she entered the place and Simon had closed the door behind her she began fumbling with the buttons of her clothes, frantic to be free of them. They made love and afterwards she lay limply beside him drifting in and out of sleep until he kissed her and said softly, "I'll take you home now."

He had sold his car so they had to walk. They didn't link arms but strolled side by side, then said goodbye at the corner of Canal Lane after arranging to meet in the park next day to discuss the latest chapters of his novel. Already she'd become proficient on the portable machine that Charlie had bought her and she was busily typing one day when Charlie became suspicious and peered at the sheaf of papers in front of her.

"What's this rubbish supposed to be?" he demanded.

When she told him that the work she was doing was for Simon, Charlie was outraged and bawled at her, "Are you taking money from that guy?"

"He hasn't got any money. I'm just doing it as a favour to a friend."

"Hasn't got any money?" Charlie sneered. "Don't they pay him anything for all the jawing he does up at that Uni?"

"He's not there now."

"Not at the Uni?"

"That's what I said."

"Where is he then?"

"Nowhere."

"What do you mean, nowhere?"

"At home."

"How can he be at home? He's still on holiday you mean? See these guys? They don't know they're born."

"No, he's resigned. He's at home writing the second draft of his novel."

"You mean to tell me he's packed in his job?"

"Yes."

"How's he keeping his wife and family?"

"Social Security."

"Social Security? National Assistance?"

"Oh, for goodness' sake, Charlie!"

"What a no-user! What a scrounger!"

"Why don't you leave him alone?"

"Why don't *you* leave him alone? I don't know what his wife must think."

"Mabel and I are friends."

"What a no-user! Can't even support his wife and family. It's guys like him that give this country a bad name."

"He's not a no-user. He's a brilliant academic. He's also a poet and an artist."

"Oh, big deal! You'd know all about how brilliant he was if you were married to him. I'm sorry for his poor wife. I bet she's glad she's got her mother and sisters and brothers all living near her. They'll be the ones that's keeping your precious poet and his wife and kids. Hard-working chaps like Jack Bannerman in Chrysler's machine shop, that's who your precious poet's wife and kids will have to depend on."

She didn't say any more. The fact was Mabel did have to accept gifts of food from her mother and other members of the family although she didn't believe Simon knew about this. Clothes for the children were also donated by Mabel's family — garments that their own youngsters had grown out of or no longer needed.

Simon eventually found out about the clothes and he had been coldly angry. He wanted Mabel to refuse the garments but Mabel insisted that on no account was she going to allow the children to be denied something they needed simply because of her pride, or his.

"He's never forgiven me for not finding myself a job and earning some money," she told Ann when they were on their own. "But I believe children need their mother in the house when they're young. I think it's terrible how kids are left on their own all day to roam the streets. Nobody knows what trouble they're getting into. No, my place is right here."

"Yes, I wouldn't have liked to leave Helen when she was young. I know how you feel."

It was true that Simon was bitter about Mabel's refusal to look for a job but to him it was only one of the many ways in which his wife had not been a helpful partner to him.

"Sometimes I feel so dragged down, Ann," he confessed. "I must have some sort of order in my life and Mabel is such a slut she nearly drives me mad."

"Oh, Simon!"

"It's the truth. If I hadn't my writing-room I couldn't stand it. You know I'm fond of her. I'm sure you are too. But could *you* live with her?"

She knew exactly what he meant. Every time she was in Mabel's flat she itched to get stuck in and get the place properly organised. Sometimes the temptation overcame her and while she was perhaps helping with the dishes she would have a quick clean-out of a cupboard stuffed with jam jars going mouldy, or rescue a bowl of sugar and other odds that had been left in passing, on a shelf of welly boots and shoes. Sometimes she would come in unexpectedly and find Simon attempting to clear a shelf or a corner of a room.

Mabel concentrated most of her time on the children. She would leave anything to sit down and talk to them or listen to them or get down on the floor with them and cover the carpet with jigsaw pieces or some other game or hobby, or material to cut out. Or she'd potter about in the kitchen baking a cake for them and spending ages over its decoration. Or she'd knit for them, sew for them, or take them out exploring in the park or along by the river. Ann supposed this was a good thing as far as the children were concerned. What did children care about a well run, tidy house?

Nevertheless she could understand how the disorder of the place depressed Simon. And of course he was in the house all the time now. Even though he shut himself away in his study for hours on end and he was acutely aware of his surroundings. The children were on holiday from school over the summer and the noise they made was also a distraction.

Often he phoned her and asked if she would meet him in the Botanic Gardens.

The day after being with him in Zoë's flat she was just leaving to meet him in the park when Helen phoned.

"Hello, dear," Ann said in surprise. "Are you calling from work?"

"No, I'm at home. I didn't go out to work this morning."

Ann alerted with apprehension. "Helen, is there anything wrong?"

"Oh, Mummy. I don't feel well."

Helen had never called her "Mummy" since she was a little girl.

"Darling! Now don't worry. I'll come right over."

142

"I've been so sick I've nearly fainted a couple of times."

"Have you glucose in the house."

"I think so."

"Try a few sips of glucose in water just now."

Charlie was at work and couldn't take her in the car so she took a taxi. This was the worst of Simon's circumstances it occurred to her as the taxi sped towards East Doltan. He wouldn't have been able to afford her bus fare to East Doltan, far less a taxi, had she been dependent on him. The thought frightened her. Money was important. There was no doubt about it in her mind. It was different for young people. A young person could try things like hitch-hiking. A young person could rough it. With youth on your side anything was possible. Without it you needed money.

It was one of the facts of life, like not being quite so physically fit as one got older. Charlie had to watch his blood pressure. These past few years if she wasn't careful she went down with an attack of tracheitis at the first cold snap of winter.

Helen peered miserably round the door in answer to her knock and immediately burst into tears at the sight of her.

"Oh, Mummy!"

"Now, now. It can't be as bad as all that."

Putting an arm around her daughter she led her into the sitting-room.

"Have you phoned your doctor?"

"No, I was hanging over the sink all the time. It was awful. But the glucose seems to have helped."

"I'll phone the doctor now, I might just catch him before he goes out on his rounds. When did the sickness start?"

"As soon as I got up this morning."

"You hadn't been eating anything last night that might have upset you?"

"No. I had exactly the same as Dave and he's all right."

Ann was pretty certain that Helen was pregnant but had confirmation from the doctor when he arrived. She didn't know whether she was gladdened by the news or not. In one way she was. Yet in another she didn't know how she was going to survive the anxiety of it all. The worry of wondering if Helen would be all right. And then if the baby would be all right. Would it never end? she thought.

But to Helen she said, "Darling, I'm so pleased. And your dad will be thrilled to bits as well. Aren't you excited?"

Helen didn't look too sure. "Yes, I suppose I am. We didn't mean to start a family just yet but still, I don't suppose Dave will mind. . . ."

"Mind? Of course he won't mind! He'll be delighted. Before the

143

words are right out of your mouth he'll be planning the kind of cot he's going to make for the baby. He'll be so proud. . . ."

"Yes." Helen began not only to perk up but look positively cheerful. "I expect he will really. I wonder what it'll be — a boy or a girl? Think of it, Mum — you'll be a granny. Can you imagine it?"

She couldn't. But she laughed and said, "I'll make a very good granny."

"Dad will make a great grandpa. But you don't look the part somehow."

"I'm not sure whether I feel flattered or insulted."

"I'm glad I feel better. That was awful this morning. I don't think I could stand any more of that."

"Take a flask of tea to bed with you at night and a few tea biscuits and the moment you waken in the morning eat a biscuit and sip a cup of tea. That used to work with me."

"OK, thanks, Mum. I'll try that. Gosh, look at the time. I'd better get something ready for Dave's lunch."

"Do you want me to make it, dear?"

"I'm OK I said, mum."

"Maybe I'd better go then and let you have your talk with Dave."

Helen did nothing to persuade her to remain and so she hurried away to catch the next bus back to the city.

It was on the journey back that she remembered her date with Simon in the park. He would have been waiting and wondering what had happened to her. She made a mental note to phone him that afternoon and explain. But when she arrived home there was a note from Simon lying on the kitchen table.

Charlie was sitting at the table grey-faced and trembling.

"What's the meaning of this?" he shouted. "This was lying behind the door when I came in just now. That middle-aged long-haired layabout has gone too far this time, Annie."

Chapter Thirty-Two

SHE THOUGHT she was going to faint. Too afraid to lift the note and see what terrible indiscretion had been committed to it she just stood staring in anguish at Charlie.

"Read it!" Charlie shouted. "Read it!"

She picked it up. Then she collapsed down on the chair. She could have laughed with relief but managed, for Charlie's sake, to stifle it. It simply said: "I will be in the park again at three pm. — Simon."

"I don't understand what you're making all the fuss about, Charlie."

144

"That long-haired layabout is making a secret assignation with you. You! My wife!"

"Oh, don't be so melodramatic. It's hardly secret when it was dropped through the letter-box like that. It's not even in an envelope. I had to meet him this morning to give him the chapters I'd typed. But I didn't turn up because I had a phone call from Helen saying she wasn't well. I had to dash straight out to East Doltan and forgot all about Simon."

"Helen?"

She could see the wind had been taken out of his sails.

"Yes, she'd been terribly sick. But don't worry, she's all right. At least, I hope she's going to be all right. She's pregnant. You're going to be a grandpa, Charlie."

His anger rapidly melted in the warmth of his delight.

"Well, I'll be. . . .! Fancy our wee girl! It seems no time since I was dandling her on my knee. And she was playing with her dolly and that red pram I bought her. Remember that wee red pram with the maroon hood?"

"Yes, she loved that, didn't she? I wonder what happened to it? Did I give it away to somebody?"

"Well, well, a grandpa, eh? He suddenly let out a loud guffaw. "You'll be a granny! An old granny, hen. What'll your brilliant poet think of you then, eh?"

She spread his lunch rolls and made a pot of tea while he continued to guffaw and gloat. He obviously thought that the fact that she was to become a granny would banish Simon from both their lives and solve all his fears about him. He never even glanced at his *Daily News,* he was enjoying himself so much. She despised him.

"Cheerio, old wife!" he chortled eventually. "Never mind, I'll treat you to a rocking chair and you can take up knitting."

The door banged behind him. She glanced at her watch. There was still plenty of time before three o'clock. She washed the dishes and put everything away thinking now about Simon waiting for her in the morning and then coming to the house and not finding her there either. He must have been worried. Poor Simon, he was anything but happy at the moment. The Social Security were beginning to really hound him. They were trying to make him take any kind of job. If he couldn't or wouldn't find a teaching job then, they said, they would classify him as a manual labourer.

"In this climate," Simon told her, "I'd die. But they are so insistent, Ann. They actually said in criticism: 'Some men *will do anything* to support their wives — even, it seems, at a wage *less* than on Social Security allowance.' To them, that seems reasonable."

To her it seemed reasonable too. But because she loved him, she didn't tell him. She believed a man *should* support his wife. But couldn't bring herself to say that either. He looked so unhappy. She loved him at that moment, protectively, loyally, as she would love a foolish child.

She checked around the house before leaving it. The cooker was switched off, and the immerser. Everything was in its proper place. Not a crumb, not a speck of dust could be seen to desecrate the velvety pile of the carpets, or the sparkling tiles of the kitchen floor. The kitchen units and even the cooker gleamed with as much pristine perfection as the day they were installed. The furniture smelled of lavender polish.

Giving the place a last glance before she shut the door, she experienced a sense of satisfaction. It was a kind of happiness.

She saw Simon before he noticed her. He was sitting on the seat in their favourite quiet corner sheltered by high rhododendron bushes and trees. He was wearing an immaculate fawn-coloured safari suit. He once told her that he pressed all his clothes himself, not trusting them to Mabel. He was meticulous about his appearance. Her heart pained her with love for him as he rose to greet her with cool, distant eyes.

"I'm sorry, darling," she said. "I had to dash over to East Doltan. Helen was ill. It turned out to be nothing serious, thank goodness. But I knew you'd already be on your way and anyway, I didn't have time to contact you."

He kissed her gently. Then they sat in silence for a time just holding hands.

"I have decided to go abroad," he said eventually.

Her heart hammered in fear against her rib-cage.

"Why should you go abroad?"

"Circumstances seem to be forcing me to take a job. And it doesn't look as if I'll be able to get a reasonable one in the UK."

She wasn't convinced. "Surely you could get another teaching post?"

"Not here. Anyway it's time I made a clean break."

"What do you mean?"

He shrugged. "I'm finding my relationship with my wife increasingly difficult to bear. Our marriage has not been working for a long time. It's been on the cards that we'd break up one day. I think it should be now."

Secretly panic-stricken she struggled to smooth calmness into her voice. "I hope this has nothing to do with me. I made it clear from the beginning that I had no intention of breaking up your marriage."

He slid her a sideways glance.

"My relationship with Mabel had deteriorated before I met you. She and I are just different kinds of people. Gradually over the years we've grown apart. We're not compatible. It's sad but there it is. There comes a time when one must face up to a situation. And *do* something about it. I believe it's time you faced up to your relationship with your marriage partner too, Ann."

"I've been married a long time."

"So have I."

"It's become a habit pattern but one that makes me feel safe, I suppose."

"Maybe that's what you need."

Miserably she hesitated. "I don't know."

"I would like you to go with me. But I have no wish to persuade you or influence you in any way. It must be your own decision — freely taken."

"I love you, Simon. But. . . ."

She struggled unsuccessfully to understand the wariness that was making her mind shrink protectively into itself. Eventually he broke into her silence.

"But not enough."

"It's not that. . . ."

Again her concentration turned inwards, and there was another tense pause.

"I'll have to go," he said, rising. "Can you meet me at Zoë's next week? We can talk then."

She nodded, embarrassed by her abstraction but at a loss to pull herself out of it. Even while he kissed her, her mind hedged about. She kept asking herself what was she afraid of. Was it because there might be financial insecurity with Simon? Was it the vision of perhaps being left to fend for herself on some strange African shore? Could she fend for herself anywhere for that matter? One had to be practical. If Simon could justify to himself leaving his wife and four children — and as far as she could see, leaving them penniless — the chances were he would find it even easier to leave a mistress if the occasion arose. At least Mabel had her mother and brothers and sisters to help her and support her if necessary. But what would she do?

Certainly she was now skilled in using a typewriter but a lot of good that would be in the middle of some God-forsaken jungle. Anyway, she'd seen advertisements in the employment agencies for staff. They were all for young women. One day she'd sat in a café opposite an agency and watched the applicants streaming in and out. There hadn't been one, not one mature woman among them. They were all mere slips of girls — far younger even than Helen.

Her mind was still going round and round in worrying circles

147

when Mabel made one of her unexpected visits.

"You're just in time for a cup of tea," Ann welcomed her, feeling sick at heart. "I was just going to pour one for myself."

"Christ," said Mabel, flinging off the fringed, multi-coloured shawl she was wearing, "this house gets more perfect every time I see it."

"Never mind the house. Sit down and have a cup of tea. Help yourself to a biscuit. Were you out shopping?"

"No, duckie, I came specially to see you."

"Oh?" Ann said cautiously. "That's nice."

In the agonizing silence that followed, Mabel gave one of her abrupt laughs and shook her head.

"Thanks, I will have a biscuit. Well?"

"Well, what?"

"Aren't you going to ask me what's wrong?"

"If you want me to."

"Oh, Christ."

"All right, what's wrong?"

"Simon's going abroad. To Saudi Arabia."

"Saudi Arabia?"

"Yes, duckie, well may you look aghast. Think of the heat, the desert, the bloody chauvinistic pigs of Arabs. You can't even get a drink out there."

"You don't want to go with him?"

"You know bloody well that I don't want to go to Saudi Arabia. But I'll tell you something else. *He* doesn't want me to go to Saudi Arabia. Now there's a thing!"

Miserably Ann avoided her eyes. "That's between you and Simon."

"Oh, is it? I wonder. I've had plenty of bad patches with him before. But somehow I've always muddled through and hung on. This time it's different. Our marriage is finished, he says. Of course, we'll be frightfully civilized and remain good friends. Simon is a very civilized man."

"Why are you telling me all this?"

"I'm buggered if I know, duckie," Mabel said, helping herself to another biscuit.

Chapter Thirty-Three

SHE NEEDED to be alone to think. But later she incurred Charlie's righteous indignation when she tried to get out of their usual night at the pub.

"I don't know what more I can do for you," he flapped up his hands, at the same time shaking his head. "I give you breakfast in bed. I give you a raise in your wages. I even gave you a type-writer. . . ."

"Charlie . . ." she began. Then, "Oh, what's the use."

There never was any point in arguing with him. It never achieved anything. If she wouldn't go to the pub, Charlie wouldn't go to the pub and his misery would be too much to bear. Going with him would be easier.

For a few minutes, though, she thought she was going to have a legitimate excuse when Helen and Dave arrived unexpectedly at the door.

"Helen! Dave! What a lovely surprise. Come on in. I'm just making the dinner. I'll put an extra couple of chops under the grill. And I've plenty of rice pudding."

"We were in town doing some shopping, Mum."

"Thought we'd just drop by," said Dave.

"Hello, Dad. Don't worry, we won't stay long. We know this is your and Mum's night out."

"Stay as long as you like, dear," Ann encouraged.

"Yes," Charlie agreed. "Relax. You've plenty of time. We don't go out until the back of eight at the earliest."

Helen tossed her coat across a chair and floped down with legs out-stretched.

"Isn't the price of everything awful, Mum? The price of children's clothes! My God! I can see me having to work up till the very last minute."

Ann looked at her sharply. "Are you sure you're fit enough to be working?"

"Oh, Mum."

"Your health comes first, remember."

"I'd be bored to death in the house all day."

Charlie puffed contentedly at his pipe. "You'll just have to get used to it when the youngster arrives."

Helen kicked off her shoes and wriggled her toes. "There's always nurseries. Or baby-minders."

"Helen! Ann was shocked. "You surely wouldn't trust your baby to complete strangers. Your own child."

"*My* child, Mum. My *own* child. I'm warning you. I don't want any interference."

"Oh, shut up," said Dave. "We might be glad of your mother as a babysitter yet."

Helen straightened up, eyes diamond hard, "Don't you tell me to shut up. Don't you dare!"

But Dave had turned to Charlie, "Did you see the match?"

"I was glued to the box. A good game, eh?"

Ann touched Helen's arm. "Come on through to the kitchen and keep me company while I'm seeing to the chops."

Helen followed her through, her stockinged feet padding on the kitchen linoleum.

"Did you hear the way he spoke to me?"

"I don't think he meant to be unkind."

"It's all very well for you to talk. You're not married to the pig!"

"Helen!"

"Well, it's true. It's easy enough for you to think he's a blue-eyed boy who can do no wrong."

"I don't think Dave's a blue-eyed boy who can do no wrong. I wish you'd sit down. You're getting in my way."

"I suppose I've always got in your way. That's why you were so keen for me to get married."

"Helen, what nonsense."

"You were, weren't you?"

"I worried about you. You seemed to get into such strange company at times. Could you blame me for getting a bit anxious?"

"Yes, Mum, I could. It was none of your damn business."

Suddenly Ann swung round on the girl. "So I'm not bloody perfect. Well, I've news for you, smart-ass, neither are you. It's about time somebody told you to shut up."

For a moment Helen was startle-eyed with shock. Then, face crumpling, she rushed howling from the kitchen.

Ann struggled with her own hysteria as she tested the chops with a fork, stirred the gravy and poured the potatoes and sprouts. Charlie strode indignantly into the kitchen just as she'd begun to dish the meal on to the plates.

"What have you been doing to our Helen?"

"I've got a splitting headache. Here, take this tray through. I'll bring the extra cutlery and dishes."

"I've told you before and I'll tell you again. . . . "

"No doubt —"

"That Uni crowd's having a bad influence on you."

"The chops are getting cold."

"Now you're even turning against your own daughter."

Lifting the other tray she pushed past him and went through to the room. The television was still on and Helen was still howling. Ann switched off the set.

"Here!" Charlie roared in protest.

"What did you say to my wife?" Dave wanted to know.

"Nothing that didn't need saying. Now sit down and eat your dinner all of you before it gets cold."

Going over to Helen she made to put her arms around the sobbing figure to pull the head comfortingly against her body as

150

she'd done so many times when Helen was a child. Child of her body, born in this very house with sweat and grunts and muffled screams. She remembered with a pang, the tiny mouth sucking at her breast.

"Leave me alone!" Helen jerked away.

Switching the television back on Charlie said, "Do you not think you've done enough harm?"

Ann found her chair and began forcing down mouthfuls of food. Helen looked so pale and sickly. What if there was something wrong with her?

"Eat up your greens like a good girl," she managed, "and I'll fetch you some nice rice pudding."

Suddenly both Helen and Dave choked with laughter. Helen spluttered out to Dave, "I told you, didn't I? She'll always treat me like a child.'"

They stayed until after "Coronation Street". Then Helen gave Charlie a kiss and a hug.

"Time for you and Mum's night out, Dad. Be good now. Don't do anything I wouldn't do."

"You've already done it," Charlie guffawed then chewed happily at the stem of his pipe.

"Well," said Helen, "if you can't be good be careful. Cheerio, Dad. Cheerio, Mum." She gave Ann a quick kiss. "Be seeing you."

"Come on," said Charlie after they'd gone. "We don't want to be late."

He linked arms with her going down the stairs. He was happy.

"Hello there, Darby and Joan," Willy Hennessy greeted them as soon as they entered the lounge bar.

"Our Helen turned up unexpectedly. Didn't stay long enough for the wife though."

"You must miss her, Mrs Sommerville," said Sadie.

"The usual, hen?" Willy winked at Ann.

"Yes," Charlie answered. "A pint of heavy for me and a sherry for her."

Chapter Thirty-Four

ANN OPENED the door and stepped into Zoë's untidy hall. A couple of empty milk bottles lay on their side on a nest of abandoned tights. A dirty wine glass balanced on a chair nearby. From the back of the chair, a hump of assorted garments, coats, dresses and a long scarf trailed on to the floor. Dust rested everywhere undisturbed.

The sitting-room carpet was awash with glasses, coffee cups,

151

dinner plates, cigarette packets and crumbs of food. The settee and chairs sagged as if under the weight of invisible people.

She tried the spare room and found that it had escaped the worst of the dinner-party of the night before. Automatically she began tidying it; hanging clothes away in cupboards, emptying ashtrays and smoothing up the bed. As she did so she caught sight of herself in the mirror above the cluttered dressing-table. What struck her was how neat and cool and efficient she looked. Her appearance gave no clue to her fevered mind. There she was, calmly emptying ashtrays and making beds just as if Simon had never said anything about going away, just as if she would go on meeting him here for the rest of her life. It was then she realized that whether or not Simon was going away, she had to make a decision.

It was a lovely romantic idea to run off to the other end of the world with a charmer like Simon, but she believed she had to be realistic and face facts. Simon's charm would never be something exclusively aimed at her. He loved her but he had loved many other women and the chances were he would love many more.

The question seemed always to boil down to: could she *depend* on Simon and the answer in her heart was always the same. She couldn't. Not in the way she had always depended on a man. But had she been right in being so utterly dependent on a man or on anyone? She had looked up to Charlie when she first met and married him and she had accepted his assessment of not only what the pattern of her life ought to be but also the type of person she was. Just as she'd done with her mother and sister. Her sister had treated her as if she was stupid and she had accepted this image of herself. Her mother had believed she was guilty of causing her sister's death and in her heart of hearts she had believed it too.

Now, for the first time, thanks to Simon, she was questioning all of these things. How ironic that he should be the key to the opening of this new door in her mind and that through it she would question him too. But then, he had opened so many doors for her. One thing she was perfectly sure of. No matter what happened, she would be eternally grateful for knowing him. He had given her an excitement for life and for her own potential. He had given her enlightenment, experience, even courage.

Nevertheless, there was still a secret confusing maze inside herself that he could not reach. She would have to find her way out of that alone.

She was tidying Zoë's sitting-room and thinking, despite her distress, of how the room could be improved by a scatter of brightly-coloured cushions, when she heard Simon arrive. She stood very still when he entered the room as if one tiny movement might allow a torrent of emotion to escape. But despite her stillness

152

tears overflowed.

"You're not coming," he said.

"No, darling. I'm not coming."

He sauntered over to the trolley and poured himself a drink, but not before she had seen the way his features collapsed into a spasm of bitterness.

Shaken, she said, "I'm sorry."

"Don't be." He turned such a calm face towards her, she thought she must have imagined the trauma of a moment before.

"You're a free individual. I respect your decision."

Her relief knew no bounds.

"Simon, you do my heart good. You do me good right to the very soul of me. I can never thank you enough."

He sipped his drink, smiled half to himself and shook his head without looking at her. Then he came across to her in that casual, arrogant way he had.

"There's no reason why we can't still be friends. Let's walk back through the park."

They strolled in silence. At last he said, "So you're going to take my advice? You're going to enrol at the University?"

It had never entered her mind. At least, not her conscious mind. But now, incredibly, she thought, "Why not?" And immediately the doors of a new world swung open. It was hard to contain her excitement.

"I might," she said.

"You'll enjoy it."

"I've so much to learn."

"Bon voyage."

She smiled fleetingly round at him. "Thank you."

When they reached the park gates, he said, "I'll send you my new address."

"Yes, I'd like to keep in touch."

"Goodbye, Ann."

"Goodbye, Simon."

And so they parted and went their separate ways as pleasantly and as casually as if they'd been doing no more than having a stroll.

It was not until she was encased in the empty box of her home that she wept and grieved for him. It wasn't that she regretted her decision. Only that it had to be this way.

Charlie arrived at the same time as usual. The loose floorboards in the hall ground under his heavy tread as he made for the bathroom. Then he lumbered into the kitchen and hung up his jacket behind the door.

"What's for dinner?"

She told him.

153

"There's a Western on tonight," he said. "I like a good Western."

He had switched on the box before she followed him through to the room. Automatically he forked food into his mouth while watching the news.

Her impatience was like a pain, she could hardly endure it. She was neither interested in the television nor the food.

After the meal Charlie loosened his tie, undid the top button of his shirt and settled down to enjoy his pipe and Randolph Scott.

She went over and switched off the set.

"What do you think you're doing?" Charlie howled in protest and lunged forward to switch it on again.

"I want to talk to you, Charlie."

"Talk to me while the commercials are on. Can't you see I'm watching the film?"

"It's important that we talk."

"Will you get out of the way of that screen?"

"It's really important, Charlie."

"OK, OK, but later. Later."

She shrugged. "It's a free country and it's your life."

"That's right. Now sit down and shut up!"

"No. When you're ready to talk I'll be at Zoë's."

He was away with the galloping horses but he called to her as she left the room.

"You can't walk up there in the dark and you're not getting a lift so forget it."

She went into the bedroom, packed a case and collected her typewriter. Back in the hall, heart skittering with apprehension, she picked up the car keys from the hall table. The racket of gunfire in the sitting-room drowned the sound of the opening and shutting of the front door. She went downstairs and, willing herself to keep calm, she put her case, typewriter and handbag into the car. Sitting behind the steering-wheel, she took a deep, deep breath before turning the key in the ignition. In a minute she had the car moving forward.

She felt she had begun an awesome and dangerous adventure. It was like being born again.